There was Susie's doll safe and sound.　See page 104.

UNCLE WIGGILY'S AUTOMOBILE

By
HOWARD R. GARIS

AUTHOR OF

Uncle Wiggily's Airship; Uncle Wiggily on the Farm; Uncle Wiggily's Travels; Uncle Wiggily's Story Book

ILLUSTRATED BY ELMER RACHE

UNCLE WIGGILY
Reg. U. S. Pat. Off:

·NEW·YORK·
·THE·PLATT·&·MUNK·C⁰·INC·

PUBLISHERS NOTE

The stories herein contained appeared originally in the Evening News, of Newark, N. J., where (so many children and their parents have been kind enough to say) they gave pleasure to a number of little folks and grown-ups also. Permission to issue the stories in book form was kindly granted by the publisher and editor of the News, to whom the author extends his thanks.

CONTENTS

Contents

Uncle Wiggily's Automobile

STORY I

UNCLE WIGGILY AND THE SORROWFUL CROW

ONCE upon a time, a good many years ago, there was an old rabbit gentleman named Uncle Wiggily Longears. He was related to Johnnie and Billie Bushytail, the squirrels, as well as being an Uncle to Sammie and Susie Littletail, his rabbit nephew and niece. And Uncle Wiggily lived near Jackie and Peetie Bow Wow, the puppy dogs, while, not far away was the home of the Wibblewobble family of ducks, and across the street, almost, around the corner by the old stump, were the Kat children, and Neddie and Beckie Stubtail, the nice bear children.

One day Uncle Wiggily was not feeling very well, so he sent for Dr. Possum, who soon came over. Dr. Possum found Uncle Wiggily sitting in the rocking chair on the front porch of the hollow stump house where he lived.

"Well, what is the trouble, Uncle Wiggily?" asked Dr. Possum, as he looked over the tops of his glasses.

"I am sick," answered the rabbit gentleman.

"Sick; eh?" exclaimed Dr. Possum. "Let me see. Put out your tongue!"

Uncle Wiggily did so.

"Ha! Hum!" exclaimed Dr. Possum. "Yes, I think you are ill, and you will have to do something for it right away."

"What will I have to do?" asked Uncle Wiggily, anxious-like, and his nose twinkled like a star on a frosty night.

"You will simply have to go away," said Dr. Possum. "There is no help for it."

"I don't see why!" exclaimed Uncle Wiggily, and he bent one of his long ears forward and the other backward, until he looked as if he had the letter V on top of his head. But, of course, he hadn't, for that letter is in the reading book—or it was the last time I looked.

"Yes," said Dr. Possum, "you must go away."

"I don't see why," said Uncle Wiggily again. "Couldn't I get well at home here?"

"No, you could not," replied Dr. Possum.
"If you want me to tell you the truth——"

"Oh, always tell the truth!" exclaimed Uncle
Wiggily, quickly. "Always!"

"Well, then," said Dr. Possum, as he looked
in his medicine case, to see if he had any strong
peppermint for Aunt Jerushia Ann, the little,
nervous old lady woodchuck. "Well, then, to
tell you the truth, you are getting too fat, and
you must take more exercise."

"Exercise!" cried Uncle Wiggily. "Why!
Don't I play a game of Scotch checkers with
Grandfather Goosey Gander, the old gentleman duck, nearly every day? And we always
eat the sugar cookies we use for checkers."

"That's just it," said Dr. Possum, as he rolled
up a sweet sugar-pill for Sammie Littletail, the
small rabbit boy; "you eat too much, and you
don't jump around enough."

"But I used to," said Uncle Wiggily, while
he twinkled his pink nose like a red star on a
frosty night. "Why, don't you remember the
time I went off and had a lot of adventures, and
how I traveled after my fortune, and found it?"

"That is just the trouble," spoke Dr. Possum.
"You found your fortune, and since you became
rich you do nothing. I remember the time when
you used to teach Sammie and Susie Littletail

how to keep out of traps, and how to dig burrows and watch out for savage dogs."

"Ah, yes!" sighed Uncle Wiggily. "Those were happy days."

"And healthful days, too," said Dr. Possum. "You were much better off then, and not so fat."

"And so you think I had better start traveling again?" asked Uncle Wiggily, taking off his high hat and bowing politely to Uncle Lettie, the nice goat lady, who was passing by, with her two horns sticking through holes in her Sunday-go-to-meeting bonnet.

"Yes, it would be the best thing for you," spoke Dr. Possum. "Medicine is all right sometimes, but fresh air, and sunshine, and being out-of-doors, and happy and contented, and helping people, as Uncle Booster, the old ground hog gentleman, used to do—all these are better than medicine."

"How is Uncle Booster, by the way?" inquired the rabbit gentleman.

"Fine! He helped a little girl mouse to jump over a mud puddle the other day, and after she was on the other side she jumped back, all by herself, and fell in," said Dr. Possum, with a laugh. "That's the kind of a gentleman Uncle Booster is!"

"Ha! Ha!" exclaimed Uncle Wiggily. "That's queer! But now do you think it would do me any good to start off and have some adventures in my automobile?"

"It would be better to walk," said Dr. Possum. "Remember you called me in to tell you what was the matter with you, because you felt ill. And I tell you that you must go around more; take more exercise. Still, if you had rather go in your auto than walk, I have no objections."

"I had much rather," said Uncle Wiggily. "I like my auto."

"Then," said Dr. Possum, "I will write that as a prescription." So on a piece of white birch bark he wrote:

"One auto ride every day, to be taken before meals.   Dr. Possum."

"I'll do it at once," said the rabbit gentleman.

Uncle Wiggily Longears was a quite rich, you know, having found his fortune, of about a million yellow carrots, as I have told you in some other stories, so he could afford to have an auto.

And it was the nicest auto you could imagine. It had a turnip for a steering wheel, and whenever Uncle Wiggily got hungry he could take a bite of turnip. Sometimes after a long trip the steering wheel would be all eaten up, and old Circus Dog Percival, who mended broken autos, would have to put on a new wheel.

And to make a noise, so that no one would get run over by his machine, Uncle Wiggily had a cow's horn fastened on his auto; so instead of going "Honk-honk!" like a duck, it went "Moo! Moo!" like a bossy cow at supper time.

"Well, if I'm going off for my health, I'd better start," said Uncle Wiggily, as he went out to his auto after Dr. Possum had gone. "I'll take a long ride."

So he got in the machine, and pushed on the doodle-oodle-um, and twisted the tinkerum-tankerum, and away he went as fast as anything, if not faster.

Over the fields and through the woods he went, and pretty soon he came to a place where lived a sorrowful crow gentleman. The crow is a black bird, and it pulls up corn and goes "Caw! Caw! Caw!" Nobody knows why, though.

And this crow was very sorrowful. He was always thinking something unpleasant was going to happen, such as that he was going to drop his ice cream cone in the mud, or that somebody would put whitewash on him. Oh, he was very sorrowful, was this crow, and his name was Mr.

Caw-caw. When Uncle Wiggily got to where the crow was sitting in a tree the black creature cried:

"Oh, dear! O woe is me! O unhappiness!"

"Why, what is the matter?" asked Uncle Wiggily, curious-like!

"Oh, something is going to happen!" cried the crow. "I know it will rain or snow or freeze, or maybe my feathers will all blow off."

"Don't be silly!" said Uncle Wiggily. "You just come for an auto ride with me, and you'll feel better. Come along, bless your black tail!"

So Mr. Caw-caw got into the auto, and once more Uncle Wiggily started off. He had not gone very far before, all of a sudden, there was a bangity-bang noise, and the auto stopped so quickly that Uncle Wiggily and the crow were almost thrown out of their seats.

"There!" cried the black crow. "I knew something would happen!" and he cried "Caw! Caw! Caw!"

"It is nothing at all," said the rabbit gentleman as he got out to look. "Only the whizzicum-whazzicum has become twisted around the jump-over-the-clothes basket, and we can't go until it's fixed."

"Can't go?" asked the crow.

"Can't go—no," said Uncle Wiggily. And

he didn't know what to do. But just then along came Old Dog Percival, who used to work in a circus.

" I'll pull you along," he said. " You sit in the auto and steer, and I'll pull you." And he did, by a rope fast to the car. The crow said it was funny to have a circus dog pulling an auto, but Uncle Wiggily did not mind, and soon they were at a place where the auto could be fixed. So Uncle Wiggily and the crow waited there, while the machine was being mended.

" And we will see what happens to us to-morrow," said Uncle Wiggily, " for I am going to travel on." And he did. And in case the jumping rope doesn't skip over the clock, and and make the hands tickle the face I'll tell you next about Uncle Wiggily and the school teacher.

STORY II

UNCLE WIGGILY LONGEARS, the nice old gentleman rabbit, was riding along in his automobile, with the turnip for a steering wheel, and he
had not yet taken more than two bites out of the
turnip, for it was only shortly after breakfast.
With him was Mr. Caw-caw, the black crow
gentleman.

"Do you think your automobile will go all
right now?" asked the crow, as he looked down
from his seat at the big wheels which had German sausages around for tires, so in case Old
Percival, the circus dog, got hungry, he could
eat one for lunch.

"Oh, yes, it will go all right now," said the
rabbit gentleman. " Specially since we have had
it fixed."

I think, if I am not mistaken, and in case the
cat has not eat up all the bacon, that I told you
in the story before this one how Uncle Wiggily

had been advised by Dr. Possum to go traveling around for his health and how he had started off in the auto. Did I tell you that?

He met Mr. Caw-caw and the tinkle-inkle-um on the auto broke, or else it was the widdle-waddle-um. Anyhow, it wouldn't go, and Old Dog Percival, coming along, pulled the machine to the fixing place. Then Uncle Wiggily and Mr. Caw-caw slept all night and now it was daylight again and they had started off once more.

" It is a lovely morning," said Uncle Wiggily, as he drove the machine over the fields and through the woods. " A lovely spring day! "

" But we may get an April shower before night," said Mr. Caw-caw, the crow gentleman, who had black feathers and who was always sad instead of being happy. " Oh, dear, I'm sure it will rain," he said.

" Nonsensicalness! " cried Uncle Wiggily, swinging his ears around just like some circus balloons trying to get away from an elephant eating peanuts. " Cheer up! Be happy! "

" Well, if it doesn't rain it will snow," said the sad crow.

" Oh, cheer up," said Uncle Wiggily, as he took another bite out of the turnip steering wheel. " Have a nibble," he went on politely. " It may only blow,"

"I'm sure it will do something," spoke the gloomy crow. "Anyhow I don't care for turnip."

"Have some corn then," said Uncle Wiggily.

"Is it popped?" asked the crow.

"No, but I can pop it," said the old gentleman rabbit. "I will pop it on my automobile engine, which gets very hot, almost like a gas stove."

So the old rabbit gentleman, who was riding around in his auto to take exercise, because he was getting too fat, and Dr. Possum had said so, popped the corn on the hot engine, and very good it was, too, for the crow to eat.

But even the popcorn could not seem to make the unhappy crow feel better, and he cried so much, as the auto went along, that his tears made a mud-puddle in the road where they happened to be just then. And the auto wheels, with the German bologna sausages on for tires, splashed in the mud and made it fly all over like anything.

Then, just as Uncle Wiggily steered the auto right away from the road into a nice green wood, where the leaves were just coming out on the trees, the old gentleman rabbit heard some one saying:

"Oh, dear! Oh, dear me! I know I'll never

be at school on time! Oh, what a bad accident!"

"My!" cried Uncle Wiggily. "What can that be?"

"Oh, something dreadful, you may be sure," said Mr. Caw-caw, the crow gentleman. "Oh, I just knew something would happen on this trip."

"Well, let it happen!" said Uncle Wiggily. "I like things to happen. This seems to be some one in trouble, and I am going to help, whoever it is."

"Then please help me," said the voice.

"Who are you?" asked Uncle Wiggily.

"I am the lady mouse school teacher," said some one they could not see, "and on my way to school I ran a thorn in my foot, so I cannot walk. If I am not there on time to open the school, the children will not know what to do. Oh, isn't it terrible!"

"Say no more!" cried Uncle Wiggily, cheerfully. "You shall ride to school in my auto. Then you will be there on time, and the animal children will not have to go home and miss their lessons. I am so glad I can help you. Isn't it horribly jolly to help people?" cried Uncle Wiggily to the crow, just as an English rabbit might have done.

"Ha! It's jolly, all right, if you can help them," said the crow. "But I'm sure something will happen. Some bad elephant will eat off our sausage tires, or a cow will drink the gasoline, or we shall roll down a hill."

" Nonsensicalness! " cried Uncle Wiggily, real exasperated-like, which means bothered. " Get in, Miss Mouse School Teacher," he said, " and I will soon have you at your classes."

So the lady mouse school teacher got into the auto, and sat beside Mr. Caw-caw, who asked her how many six and seven grains of corn were.

" Thirteen," said the nice mouse school teacher.

" Thirteen in the winter," spoke the crow, " but I mean in summer."

" Six and seven are thirteen in summer just as in winter," said the lady mouse.

" Wrong," croaked the crow. " If you plant thirteen grains of corn in summer you'll get thirteen stalks, each with thirteen ears of corn on, and each ear has five hundred and sixty-three grains, and thirteen times thirteen times five hundred and sixty-three makes—how many does it make? " he asked of Uncle Wiggily suddenly.

" Oh, please stop! " cried the lady mouse school teacher; " you make my head ache."

" How much is one headache and two headaches? " asked the crow, who seemed quite curious.

" Stop! Stop! " cried Uncle Wiggily, as he

took a bite out of the turnip steering wheel. "You will make the auto turn a somersault."

"How much," said the crow, "is one somersault and one peppersault added to a mustard plaster and divided by——"

"There you go!" suddenly cried Uncle Wiggily as the auto hit a stone and stopped. "You've made the plunkity-plunk bite the wizzie-wazzie!"

"Oh, dear!" cried the crow. "I knew something would happen!"

"Well, it was your fault," said Uncle Wiggily. "Now I'll have to have the auto fixed again."

"Can't we go on to school?" asked the lady mouse teacher anxiously.

"No, I am sorry to say, we cannot," said Uncle Wiggily.

"Then I shall be late, and the children will all run home after all. Oh, dear!"

"I knew something——" began the crow.

"Stop it!" cried Uncle Wiggily, provoked-like.

The lady mouse school teacher did not know what to do, and it looked as if she would be late, for even when Uncle Wiggily had crawled under the auto, and had put pepper on the German sausage tires, he could not make the machine go,

But, just as the school teacher was going to be late, along came flying Dickie Chip-Chip, the sparrow boy, with his new airship. And in the airship he gave the lady mouse school teacher a ride to school up above the tree tops, so she was not late after all.

She called a good-by to Uncle Wiggily, who some time afterward had his auto fixed again, and then he and the crow gentleman went on and had more adventures. What the next one was I'll tell you on the next page, when the story will be about Uncle Wiggily and the candy—that is, if a little Montclair girl, named Cora, doesn't eat too much peanut brittle, and get her hair so sticky that the brush can't comb it.

STORY III

UNCLE WIGGILY AND THE CANDY

UNCLE WIGGILY, the nice old gentleman rab bit, was riding along in his automobile, with the turnip for a steering wheel and big, fat German bologna sausages on for tires. On the seat beside Uncle Wiggily was the crow gentleman, named Mr. Caw-caw.

"Well, where do you think you will go to-day?" asked the crow gentleman, as he straightened out some of his black feathers with his black bill, for the wind had ruffled them all up.

"Where will I go?" repeated Uncle Wiggily, as he steered to one side so he would not run over a stone and hurt it, "well, to tell you the truth— I hardly know. Dr. Possum, when he told me to ride around for my health, because I was getting too fat, did not say where I was to go, in particular."

"Then let's go straight ahead," said the crow. "I don't like going around in a circle; it makes me dizzy."

"And it does me, also," spoke the rabbit

gentleman. " That is why I never can ride much on a merry-go-'round, though I often take Johnnie or Billie Bushytail, my squirrel nephews, or Buddy and Brighteyes, the guinea pig children, on one for a little while. But, Mr. Crow, we will go straight ahead in my auto, and we will see what adventure happens to us next."

For you know something was always happening to Uncle Wiggily as he traveled around. Sometimes it was one thing, and sometimes another. You remember, I dare say, how, the day before, he had nearly helped to keep the nice lady mouse school teacher from being late.

Well, pretty soon, as Uncle Wiggily and the crow gentleman were riding in the auto, all at once they looked down the road and saw a little girl sitting on a stone. She had a box in her hands and she was trying to open it. But she was crying so hard that she could not see out of her eyes, because of her tears, and so she could not open the box.

" My goodness me sakes alive, and some roast beef gravy! " cried Uncle Wiggily, as he stopped the auto. " What can be the matter with that child? " For you know Uncle Wiggily loved children.

Then the old gentleman rabbit blew on the cow's horn, that was on his auto to warn people kindly to get out of danger, and the cow's horn went " Moo! Moo! Moo!" very softly, three times just like that.

The little girl looked up through her tears, and when she saw Uncle Wiggily and the crow gentleman in the auto, she smiled and asked:

" Where is the mooley cow? "

" Only her horn is here," said Uncle Wiggily, as he made it go " Moo!" again.

" Oh, dear," said the little girl. " I just love a mooley cow," and she was going to cry some more, because there was no cow to be seen, when Uncle Wiggily asked:

" What is the matter? Why are you crying? "

" Because I can't get this box open," said the little girl, whose name was Cora.

" What is in the box? " asked the rabbit gentle-man.

" Candy," said little Cora. " I just love candy, and I haven't had any in ever so long. Now my papa gave me a box, but the string is tied on it so tightly that I can't get the box open, and my papa went away and forgot about it. Oh, dear. Boo! hoo! Can you open it for me, Uncle Wiggily? "

The rabbit gentleman thought for a moment. Then he said, with a twinkle in his eyes that matched the twinkle in his nose:

"Well, possibly I might untie the string, but you see my teeth are so big and sharp, and are so used to gnawing wood, and bark and carrots, and I can't see very well, even with my glasses, so I might accidentally, when I bite through the string I might, by mistake, also bite through the box, and eat the candy myself."

"Oh, dear!" cried the little girl. Then she added quickly, as she thought of her polite manners: "I wouldn't mind, Uncle Wiggily, if you did eat some of the candy. Only open the box for me so I can get part of it," she said.

"I think I have a better plan that that," said the old gentleman rabbit. "I will ask Mr. Caw-caw, our crow friend here, to untie the string for you. With his sharp bill this crow gentleman can easily loosen the knot, and that, too, without danger of breaking the box and taking any candy."

"Will he do it?" asked the little girl eagerly.

"To be sure, I will," said the crow gentleman, and he loosened that knot then and there with his sharp bill, which seemed just made for such things.

"Oh, what lovely candy!" cried the little girl, as she took the cover off the box. "I am going to give you each some!" she added. And she gave Mr. Caw-caw some candy flavored with

green corn, for he liked that best of all, and to
Uncle Wiggily she gave some nice, soft, squishie-
squashie candy, with a carrot inside. And the
little girl ate some chocolate candy for herself,
and did not cry any more.

"Get in my auto," said Uncle Wiggily, " and
I will give you a ride. Perhaps we may have an
adventure."

"Oh, I just love adventures!" said little Cora.
"I love them even better than candy. But we
can eat candy in the auto anyhow," she went on,
with a laugh, as she climbed up in the seat.

Then Uncle Wiggily turned the tinkerum-
tankerum, and with a feather tickled the whizzicum-whazzicum to make the auto go, and it
went. The old rabbit gentleman made the cow's
horn blow "Moo! Moo!" and away they started
off through the woods.

They had not gone very far, and Cora had
eaten only about six pieces of candy, when they
heard a voice behind them shouting:

"Wait for me! Wait for me! I want a ride!"

"Ha!" cawed the crow, "who can that be?"

"I'll look," said Uncle Wiggily, and he did.
Then he exclaimed: "Oh, dear! It's the circus
elephant. And he's grown so big lately, that if
he gets in with us he will break my auto."

"Don't let him do it then," said Mr. Caw-caw

"I don't believe I will," said Uncle Wiggily.

"But would it be polite not to give him a ride?" asked the little girl, as she ate another piece of candy.

"No, you are right, it would not," said Uncle Wiggily, decidedly. "I must give him a ride, but he's sure to break my auto, and then I can't ride around for my health any more, and stop getting fat. Oh, dear, what a predicament!" A predicament means trouble, you know.

Then the elephant called again:

"I say, hold on there! I want a ride!" and he came on as fast as anything. Uncle Wiggily was going to stop, and let the big creature get in, when the crow gentleman said:

"I have it! We'll pretend we don't hear him. We'll keep right on, and not stop, and then it won't be impolite, for he will think we didn't listen to what he said."

"That's it," said Uncle Wiggily. "We'll do that. Pachy is the dearest old chap in the world, you know, but he really is too big for this auto." Pachy was the elephant's name, you see.

So Uncle Wiggily made the auto go faster, and still the elephant ran after it, calling:

"Stop! Stop! I want a ride!"

"He's catching up to us," said the crow, looking back.

"Oh, dear!" cried Uncle Wiggily, "what's to be done?"

"I know what to do," spoke Cora. "I'll drop some pieces of candy in the road for him, and when he stops to eat them we can get so far away he can't catch up to us."

"Please do," begged Uncle Wiggily, and the little girl did. And when the elephant saw the pieces of candy, being very fond of sweet things, he stopped to pick them up in his trunk and eat them.

And it took him quite a while, for the candy was well scattered about. And when the elephant had eaten the last piece Uncle Wiggily and the crow, and little girl, were far off in the auto and the elephant could not catch them to break the machine; though even if he had smashed it he would not have meant to do so.

So Uncle Wiggily rode on, looking for more adventures, and he soon found one. I'll tell you about it in the next story, which will be called, "Uncle Wiggily at the Squirrel House;"—that is if the clothes wringer doesn't squeeze the rubber ball so it cries and makes water come in the eyes of the potatoes.

STORY IV

UNCLE WIGGILY AT THE SQUIRREL HOUSE

UNCLE WIGGILY, the nice old gentleman, rabbit, was standing one day in front of his new automobile which had run away with him upsetting, and breaking one of the wheels. But it had been fixed all right again.

"I think this automobile will go fine now," said Uncle Wiggily to himself, as he got up on the front seat. "Now, I am ready to start off on some more travels, and in search of more adventures, and this time I won't have to walk. Now let me see, do I turn on the fizzle-fazzle first or the twinkum-twankum? I forget."

So he looked carefully all over the automobile to see if he could remember what first to turn to make it go, but he couldn't think what it was. Because, you see, he was all excited over his accident. I didn't tell you that story because I thought it might make you cry. It was very sad. The crow gentleman flew away after it.

"I guess I'll have to look in the cookbook," said Uncle Wiggily. "Perhaps that will tell me what to do."

So he took out a cookbook from under the seat and leafed it over until he came to the page where it tells how to cook automobiles, and there he found what he wanted to know.

"Ha! I see!" cried Uncle Wiggily; "first I must twist the dinkum-dankum, and then I must tickle the tittlecum-tattlecum, and then I'll go."

Well, he did this, and just as he was about to start off on his journey out came running Sammie and Susie Littletail, the two rabbit children, with whom Uncle Wiggily sometimes lived.

"Oh, Uncle Wiggily!" cried Susie, "where are you going?"

"And may we come along?" asked Sammie, making his nose twinkle like two stars on a night in June.

"I am going off on a long journey, for my health, and to look for more adventures," said the old gentleman rabbit. "I am tired of staying around the house taking medicine for my rheumatism. So Dr. Possum told me to travel around. I don't just know where I am going, but I am going somewhere, and if you like you may come part of the way. Hop in."

Sammie and Susie hopped in the back part of

the auto, where there were two little seats for
them, and then Uncle Wiggily turned the
whizzicum-whazzicum around backward and
away they went as nicely as the baby creeps over
the floor to catch the kittie by the tail; only you
mustn't do that, you know; indeed not!

" Oh, isn't this great? " cried Susie, in delight.

" It certainly is," agreed Sammie, blinking his
pink eyes because the wind blew in them. " I
hope Uncle Wiggily has an adventure while
we're with him."

And then, all of a sudden, a doggie ran across
the road in front of the auto, and the doggie's
tail was hanging down behind him and sticking
out quite a bit, and, as it was quite a long tail,
Uncle Wiggily nearly ran over it, but, of course,
he didn't mean to, even if he had done it.

" Look out of the way, little doggie! " cried the
old gentleman rabbit, kindly.

" I am looking as fast as I can! " cried the
doggie, and he ran to the sidewalk as quickly as
he could, and then he turned around to see if his
tail was still fastened to him.

" That came near being an adventure," said
Susie, waving her pocket handkerchief.

" Yes, almost too near," said Uncle Wiggily.
" I think I will go through the woods instead of

along the streets, and then I won't be in any danger of running over any one."

So he steered the auto toward the woodland road, and Sammie cried:

"Oh, I know what let's do! Let's go call on Johnnie and Billie Bushytail, the squirrel boys. Then we'll have some fun."

"All right, we'll do it," agreed Uncle Wiggily, for he liked fun as much as the children did, if not more.

Well, as they were going along the road, all of a sudden they heard a little voice calling to them.

"Oh, please don't run over me!" the voice cried. "Please be careful!" And, looking down, Sammie saw a little black cricket on the path just ahead of the auto, which Uncle Wiggily was now making go very slowly.

"Why don't you get out of the way if you don't want to be run over?" asked Susie, politely, for the cricket just stood still there, looking at them, and not making a move.

"Oh, I'm so stiff from the cold that I can't hop about any more," said the cricket, "or else I would hop out of the way. You know I can't stand cold weather."

"That's too bad," said Uncle Wiggily as he stopped the auto. "I'll give you a ride, and perhaps I can find some warm place for you to spend the winter."

So the old gentleman rabbit kindly picked up the cold and stiff cricket and gave it to Susie, and Susie gently put it in the warm pocket of her jacket, and there it was so nice and cozy-ozy that the cricket went fast to sleep.

And then, in about forty-'leven squeak-squawk toots of the big mooley-cow automobile horn, there they were at the home of Johnnie and Billie Bushytail, the squirrel brothers.

" Toot! Toot! " tooted Uncle Wiggily on his tooter-tooter mooley-cow horn.

" There! I guess that will bring out the boys if they are in the house," said the old gentleman rabbit.

And then, all of a sudden, something happened. Susie and Sammie were looking at the front door, expecting Johnnie and Billie to come out, when Susie saw a great big bear's face up at one window of the squirrel house.

" Oh! Look! Look! " she cried. " The bear has gotten in and maybe he has bitten Johnnie."

And just then Sammie looked at the other window and he saw a wolf's face peering out.

" Oh, dear! " cried Sammie, " the wolf has gotten Billie."

" My gracious! " exclaimed Uncle Wiggily.

"I'm going for the police right away. Hold on tightly, children, for I am going to twist the tinkerum-tankerum and make this automobile go very fast. Oh! how sorry I am for poor Johnnie and Billie."

But just before Uncle Wiggily could start the auto, there was a shout of laughter. The front door of the Bushytail home swung open, and out rushed Billie and Johnnie, jumping and skipping. And Johnnie had a wolf's false face in his paws and Billie had a bear's false face in his paws.

"Ho! Ho!" they shouted together. "Did we scare you, Uncle Wiggily? We didn't mean to, but we were just practising."

"Was that you boys looking out of the windows with your false faces on?" asked Uncle Wiggily very much surprised-like.

"That was us," said Johnnie.

"And wasn't there a real bear?" asked Susie, flapping her ears.

"And wasn't it a real wolf?" asked Sammie, wiggling his paws.

"Not a bit," said Billie. "We're just getting ready for Hallowe'en to-morrow night, and those were our false faces, you know, and I wish you'd all stay with us and have some fun."

"We will," said Uncle Wiggily. "I'll put my auto in the barn, and we'll stay."

So they did, and in case the little wooden dog with the pink-blue nose doesn't bite the tail of the woolly cat, I'll tell you next about Uncle Wiggily having Hallowe'en fun.

STORY V

UNCLE WIGGILY'S HALLOWE'EN FUN .

"Oh, dear, I wish it were night," said Susie Littletail.

"So do I!" exclaimed Sammie, her brother. "Then it would be Hallowe'en."

"And both of us wish the same thing," said Johnnie Bushytail, as he and his brother Billie went skipping about the room of their house.

"Oh, don't wish so hard or night might come before I'm ready for it," said Uncle Wiggily Longears, the old gentleman rabbit. "I've got to decorate my auto yet and get my false face, you know."

"What kind are you going to have?" asked Susie.

"Oh, I think I'll dress up like an elephant," said Uncle Wiggily.

"But what will you do for a trunk?" asked Mrs. Bushytail, for, you see, Uncle Wiggily and Sammie and Susie had stayed at the sqiurrel's house to have some fun. This was the first place

38

the old gentleman rabbit came to after starting out in his auto for his health, and after some fresh adventures. "What will you do for an elephant's trunk?" asked Mrs. Bushytail.

"I will take a long stocking and stuff it full of soft cotton so it will look just like an elephant's face," said Uncle Wiggily. "Then I'll go out with the children in my auto and we'll have a lot of fun."

So all that day they got ready for the Hallowe'en fun they were to have that night. Johnnie and Billie had their false faces, you remember; Johnnie had a wolf's face and Billie a bear's, and they were too cute for anything. But, of course, Sammie and Susie Littletail and Uncle Wiggily had to have some false faces also, and it took quite a while for the rabbit children to decide what they wanted.

"I think I'll dress up like a wild Indian," said Sammie at last.

"And I'm going to be a pussy cat," said Susie.

"And if any dogs chase you, I'll growl at them, and scare them away," said Billie, who was going to be a make-believe bear.

"Yes, and I'll tickle them with my stuffed-stocking elephant's trunk," said Uncle Wiggily. "Now, I must go out and put some oil and gasoline in my auto, and see that the frizzlefrazzle works all right, so we can go Hallowe'en riding to-night."

Finally the animal children were all ready, and they were waiting for it to get dark so they could go out. And, pretty soon, after supper, when the sun had gone to bed, it did get dark. Then the four animal children and Uncle Wiggily went out in the auto.

Say, I just wish you could have seen them; really I do! and I'd show you a picture of them, only I'm not allowed to do that. And besides it was too dark to see pictures well, so perhaps it doesn't much matter.

Oh, but they were the funny looking sights, though! Billy Bushytail acted like a real bear, growling as hard as ever he could, though, of course, he was polite about it, as it was only fun. And what a savage make-believe wolf Johnnie was!

And there was Susie, as cute a little pussy cat as one would meet with in going from here to the moon and back. And as for Sammie, well, say, he was so much like a real Indian that when he looked in the glass he was frightened at himself; yes, really he was, and he had truly feathers on, too; not make-believe ones, either.

Uncle Wiggily was dressed up like an elephant, and he sat in the front of the auto to steer it. Only his stuffed-stocking trunk got in the way of the steering wheel, so Uncle Wiggily had to put it behind him, over his left shoulder and have Susie hold it. I mean she held his stuffed-stocking trunk, not the steering wheel, you know.

"Here we go!" suddenly cried Uncle Wiggily, and his voice sounded far away because it had to go down inside the stuffed-stocking elephant trunk and come out again around in back of him. Then he twisted the tinkerum-tankerum, and away they went in the automobile.

All at once, from around a corner, came a big clown with red, white and blue all over his face. He had a rattlety-bang-banger thing and he was making a terrible racket on it.

"Oh, I know who that is!" cried Susie. "You're Jimmie Wibblewobble, the boy duck."

"That's right," said the clown, making more noise than ever. "Whoop-de-doodle-do! Isn't this fun!"

Along went the auto and by this time there were a whole lot of animal children prancing and dancing around it. Uncle Wiggily had to make the auto go real slowly so as not to hurt any of them, for they were all over the streets.

There was Buddy Pigg, dressed up like a camel, and there was Dickie Chip-Chip and his sister, and they were dressed up like sailors.

Brighteyes Pigg had on a cow's false face and
Billie Goat was dressed up like a Chinaman, while
Nannie, his sister, was supposed to be a lady with
a sealskin coat on. Oh, I couldn't tell you how
all the different animal children were dressed, but
I'll just say that Bully, the frog, with his tall
hat, was dressed like a football player and Aunt
Lettie, the nice old lady goat, made believe she
was a fireman, and Munchie Trot was a pretend-
policeman.

And such fun as they as they had! Uncle
Wiggily steered the auto here and there, and
squeaked and squawked his tooter-teeter so no
one would get hurt. There were about forty-
'leven tin horns being blown, and the wooden
rattlety-bang-bangs were rattling all over and
some one threw a whole lot of prettily colored
paper in the air until it looked as if it were raining red, pink, green, purple, blue, yellow and
skilligimink colored snow.

And then, all at once, out from the crowd,
came a figure that looked like a bear. Oh, it was
very real looking with long teeth, and shaggy fur,
and that bear came right up to the auto that
Uncle Wiggily was steering.

"I've come to get you!" growled the bear,
away down in his throat.

"Oh, he's almost real!" exclaimed Susie, and

she forgot that she was holding Uncle Wiggily's stuffed-stocking trunk, and let go of it, so that it hung down in front of him.

"I am a real bear!" growled the shaggy creature.

"Oh, you can't fool us," said Johnnie Bushy-tail, with a laugh. "You're Jacko or Jumpo Kinkytail dressed up like a bear, just as my brother Billie is. You can't fool us."

"But I am a real bear!" growled the shaggy creature again, "and I'm hungry so I'm going to bite Uncle Wiggily."

And, would you ever believe it? he was a real bear who had come in from the woods. He made a grab for Uncle Wiggily, but the old gentleman rabbit leaned far back in his auto seat, and the bear only got hold of the stuffed-stocking trunk. And then the bear pulled on that so hard that it came all apart and the cotton stuffing came out, and got up the bear's nose and made him sneeze.

And then up came running Munchie Trot, the pony boy, who was dressed like a policeman, and with his club Munchie tickled the bear on his ear, and that shaggy creature was glad enough to run back to the woods, taking his little stubby tail with him, so he didn't eat anybody.

"My, it's a good thing, I didn't have on a real

elephant's trunk," said Uncle Wiggily, " or that bear would have bitten it off, for real trunks are fastened on tight."

" Yes, indeed," said Susie. So after everybody got over being scared at the real bear they had a lot of fun and Uncle Wiggily took all the children to a store and treated them to hot chocolate, and then he and Sammie and Susie and Billie and Johnnie went home in the auto, and went to bed. And Uncle Wiggily had another adventure next day.

I'll tell you about it on the page after this, when, in case it doesn't rain lightning bugs down the chimney, the story will be about Uncle Wiggily going chestnutting.

STORY VI

UNCLE WIGGILY GOES CHESTNUTTING

"WHERE are you going this morning, Uncle Wiggily?" asked Johnnie Bushytail of the old gentleman rabbit the day after the Hallowe'en fun.

"Oh, I am going to take a ride and see if I can find any more adventures," said Uncle Wiggily, as he went out in the barn to look and see if his auto had any holes in the rubber tires, or if the what-you-may-call-it had gotten twisted around the whose-this-cantankerum.

"May I go with you?" asked Billie Bushytail, as he followed Uncle Wiggily. "We don't want you to go away from our house so soon. We'd like to have you pay us a nice, long visit."

"Hum, well, I'll think about it," said Uncle Wiggily, slowly, and careful-like. "I'll stay as long as I can. But as for you squirrel boys going for a ride in my auto, why I guess you may come if your mamma will let you. Yes, it's all ready for a spin," he went on, as he saw that the tiddle-

taddleum was on straight, and that the wheels
had no holes in them.

"Oh, goody! Come on!" cried Billie to
Johnnie; so into the house they hurried to ask
their mamma, and she said they might go.

A little later, with the squirrel boys sitting in
the back part of the auto, away they went, Uncle
Wiggily steering here and there and taking care
not to run over any puppy-dogs' tails or over any
alligators' noses.

"Are you going off in the woods?" asked
Johnnie, as he saw the old gentleman rabbit steering toward the tree-forest.

"I think I will," answered Uncle Wiggily.
"I want to see Grandfather Goosey Gander, and
if we go through the woods that is the shortest
way to his house."

"Then, perhaps, we can stop and gather some
chestnuts," said Johnnie. "There may be a few
left that the other squirrels haven't yet picked up,
and I heard papa saying to mamma the other
night that we need a whole lot more than we have,
so we wouldn't be hungry this winter."

"Oh, yes; let's get chestnuts!" cried Billie.

"All right," answered Uncle Wiggily, smiling, and then he had to turn the auto to one side
very quickly, for a fuzzy worm was hurrying
along the path, on her way to the grocery store,

and Uncle Wiggily didn't want to run over her, you know.

" Thank you very much for not squashing me flat like a pancake," said the worm, as she wiggled along.

" Oh, pray do not mention such a little thing," said Uncle Wiggily, politely. " I am always glad to do you a favor like that."

Then he turned the handle so some more gasoline would squirt into the fizzle-fozzleum, and away the automobile went faster than ever.

Pretty soon they came to the woods, and Johnnie and Billie began looking about for chestnut trees. Squirrels, you know, can tell a chestnut tree a great way off, and soon Johnnie saw one.

" Stop the auto here, Uncle Wiggily," said Johnnie, " and we'll see if there are any chestnuts left."

So the old gentleman rabbit did this, and, surely enough, there were quite a few of the brown nuts lying on the ground, partly covered with leaves.

" Take a stick and poke around and you'll find more," said Billie to his brother, and pretty soon all three of them, including Uncle Wiggily, were picking up the nuts. Of course, the automobile couldn't pick up any; it just had to stand still there, looking on. I guess you know that, anyhow, but I just thought I'd mention it to make sure.

"Oh, here is another tree over there!" cried Johnnie after a while, as he ran to a large one. "It's got heaps and heaps of chestnuts under it, too. I guess no squirrels or any chipmunks have been here. Oh, we can get lots of nuts to put away for winter!"

So the two squirrel boys filled their pockets with nuts, and so did Uncle Wiggily, and they even put some in the automobile, though, of course, the auto couldn't eat them, but it could carry them away. And then, all of a sudden, Billie cried:

"Oh, I know what let's do! Let's build a little fire and roast some of the chestnuts. They're fine roasted."

"I guess they are," said Uncle Wiggily, "and so we'll cook some, though, as for me, I'd rather have a roast carrot or a bit of baked apple."

"Maybe we can find some apples to bake while we're roasting the chestnuts," said Billie. "We'll look."

They looked all around, and in a field not far from the woods they found an apple tree and there were some apples on the ground under it.

They picked up quite a few and then they got some flat stones and made a place to build a fire.

Uncle Wiggily lighted it, for it isn't good for children to have anything to do with matches, and soon the fire was blazing up very nicely and was quite hot.

" Now put the chestnuts down to roast on the hot stones," said the rabbit gentleman, after a bit, to the two squirrel boys, " and I'll put some apples on a sharp stick and hold them near the blaze to roast. Why, boys! This is as much fun for me as a picnic! " he exclaimed joyfully.

But listen! Something is going to happen. All of a sudden, as they were sitting quietly around the fire and wishing the apples and chestnuts would hurry up and roast, all of a sudden a man came along with a gun. He stood by the fence that went around the field where they had picked up the apples, and that man said, in a grillery-growlery voice:

" Ah, ha! So those squirrels and that rabbit have been taking my apples, eh? I can smell 'em! Sniff! Snoof! Snuff! Well, I'll soon put a stop to that! I'm glad I brought my gun along! "

He was just aiming his gun at poor Uncle Wiggily and also at Johnnie and Billie Bushy-tail, and the rabbit and the squirrels didn't know

what in the world to do, for they were too
frightened to run, when, all of a sudden there was
a tremendously loud bang-bang in the fire and
something flew out of it and hit that man right
on the end of his nose.

" Ouch-ouchy! " the man cried.

" Bang! " went something again, and this time
it flew over and hit the man on his left ear. Now
what do you think of that?

" Ouch! Ouchy! " the man yelled again.

" Bang! " went the noise for the third shot,
and this time the man was hit on his other ear.

" Ouch! Ouchy! " he cried again. " They're
shooting at me. I'd better run." And run away
he did, taking his gun with him, and so Uncle
Wiggily and Johnnie and Billie weren't hurt.

" My, that was a narrow escape," said Johnnie.
" What was it that made the bang noise, and hit
the man? "

" It was the roast chestnuts," said Uncle Wiggily, " I forgot to tell you to make little holes in
them before you roasted them or else they would
burst. And burst they did, and I'm glad of it,
for they scared that man. But I guess we had
better be going now, for he may come back."

So they took the apples, which were nicely
roasted now, and they took the chestnuts that
were left and which hadn't burst, and away they

went in the auto and had a fine ride, before going home to bed.

And now I'll say good-night, but in case the cow who jumped over the moon doesn't kick our milk bottles off the back stoop, I'll tell you, in the story after this one, about Uncle Wiggily and the pumpkin.

STORY VII

UNCLE WIGGILY AND THE PUMPKIN

"WELL," said Uncle Wiggily Longears one fine fresh morning, just after the milkman had been around to leave some cream for the coffee, "I think I will be traveling on again, Mrs. Bushytail."

"Oh, don't go yet!" begged Billie, the boy squirrel.

"No, you haven't made us a long visit at all," spoke his brother Johnnie. "Can't you stay a long, long time?"

"Well, I promised Jimmie Wibblewobble, the boy duck, that I would come in my new automobile and pay him and his sisters a visit," said the old gentleman, as he wiggled first his left ear and then the right one to see if there were any pennies stuck in them. And he found two pennies, one for Johnnie and one for Billie.

"Oh, please stay with us a few more days. You can go visit the Wibblewobble family next week," said Johnnie; "can't he, mother?"

" Yes, I really think you might stay with us a little longer," said Mrs. Bushytail, as she was mending some holes in Johnnie's stocking. " Besides, I thought you might do me a favor to-day, Uncle Wiggily."

" A favor!" exclaimed the old gentleman rabbit, making a low bow. " I am always anxious to do you a favor if I can. What is it, Mrs. Bushytail?"

" Why, I thought you and the boys might like to go off in the automobile and see if you could find me a nice, large yellow pumpkin," said the squirrel lady.

" Oh, goody!" cried Billie. " I know what for—to make a Jack-o'-lantern for us, eh, mamma?"

" Sure!" cried Johnnie, jumping up and down because he was so happy, " and we'll take it out after dark, Billie, and have some fun with Bully the frog."

" Oh, no, not a pumpkin for a Jack-o'-lantern," said Mrs. Bushytail. " What I need a pumpkin for is to make some pies, and I thought you might like to get one, Uncle Wiggily."

" Yes, indeed, I would!" exclaimed the old gentleman rabbit. " I am very fond of hunting pumpkins for pies, and also eating them after they are baked. I like pumpkin pie almost as

much as I do cherry pie. Come on, boys, let's get
into the auto and we'll go look for a pumpkin."

" But don't go near that man's field who was
going to shoot us the other day because we took
a few apples," said Billie, and Uncle Wiggily
said he wouldn't. So out they went to the barn,
where the auto was kept, leaving Mrs. Bushytail
in the house mending stockings and getting ready
to bake the pumpkin pies.

" Here we go! " cried Uncle Wiggily, when he
had tickled the tinkerum-tankerum with a feather
to make it sneeze.

Away went the auto, and as it rolled along on
its big fat wheels Uncle Wiggily sang a funny
little song, like this:

" Pumpkin pie is my delight,
I eat it morning, noon and night,
It's very good to make you grow,
That's why the boys all love it so.

" If I could have my dearest wish,
I'd have some cherries in a dish.
And then a pumpkin pie, or two;
Of course, I'd save a piece for you.

" Perhaps, if we are good and kind,
A dozen pumpkins we may find,

We'll bring them home and stew them **up,**
And then on pumpkin pie we'll sup."

Well, after he had sung that song, Uncle Wiggily felt better. The auto felt better also, I
guess, for it ran along very fast, and, all of a
sudden, they came to a place where there was a
field of pumpkins. Oh, such lovely, large, golden
yellow pumpkins as they were.

" Hurray! " cried Johnnie.

" Whoop-de-doodle-do! " cried Billie.

" Dear me hum suz dud! " cried Uncle Wiggily. " It couldn't be better. But I wonder if
these pumpkins would mind if we took one? "

" Not in the least! Not in the least! " suddenly cried a voice near the fence, and looking
over, Uncle Wiggily and the boys saw Grandfather Goosey Gander, the old gentleman duck,
standing there on one leg. " This is my field of
pumpkins," said Grandfather Goosey, " and you
may take as many as you like." Then he put
down his other leg, which he had been holding up
under his feathers.

" Thank you very much," spoke Uncle Wiggily politely.

" And may we each have a pumpkin to make
a Jack-o'-lantern? " asked Billie.

" To be sure," answered Grandfather Goosey,

so Uncle Wiggily took a very large pumpkin for
a pie, and the boy squirrels took smaller ones for
their lanterns. Then Uncle Wiggily took a few
more to be sure he would have plenty, but none
was as large as the first one.

"I will send you some pumpkin pies when
Mrs. Bushytail bakes them," promised the old
gentleman rabbit as he got ready to travel on
with the boys in the auto.

"I wish you would," said Grandfather
Goosey, "as I am very fond of pumpkin pie
with watercress salad on top."

On and on went the auto, and Billie and
Johnnie were talking about how they would
make their Jack-o'-lanterns and have fun, when
all of a sudden, out from the bushes at the side of
the road, jumped the big, bad savage wolf.

"Hold on there!" he cried to Uncle Wiggily.
"Stop, I want to see you!"

"You want to bite me, I guess," said the old
gentleman rabbit. "No, sir! I'm not going to
stop."

"Then I'll just make you!" growled the wolf,
and with that what did he do but bite a hole in
one of the big rubber tires, letting out all the
wind with a puff, so the auto couldn't go any
more.

"Now see what you've done!" cried Johnnie.

"Yes, and it was a nice, new auto, too," said
Billie sorrowfully.

"Fiddlesticks!" cried the wolf. "Double
fiddlesticks. Don't talk to me. I'm hungry.
Get out of that auto, now, so I can bite you."

"Oh! what shall we do?" whispered Johnnie.

"Hush! Don't say a word. I'm going to
play a trick on that wolf," said Uncle Wiggily.
Then he spoke to the savage creature, saying:
"If you are going to eat us up, I s'pose you will;
but first would you mind taking one of these
pumpkins down to the bottom of the hill and
leaving it there for Mrs. Bushtail to make a pie
of?"

"Oh, anything to oblige you, since I am going
to eat you, anyhow," said the wolf. "Give me
the pumpkin, but mind, don't try to run away,
while I'm gone for I can catch you. I'll come
back and eat you up in a minute."

"All right," said Uncle Wiggily, giving the
wolf a little pumpkin, and pretending to cry, to
show that he was afraid. But he was only making believe, you see. Well, the wolf began to
run down to the foot of the hill.

"Now, quick, boys!" suddenly cried Uncle
Wiggily. "We'll roll the biggest pumpkin
down after him, and it will hit him and make

him as flat as a pancake, and then he can't eat us! Lively, now!"

So, surely enough, they took the big pumpkin out of the auto and rolled it down after the wolf. He heard it coming and he tried to get out of the way, but he couldn't, because he was carrying another pumpkin, and he stumbled and fell down, and the big pumpkin rolled right over him, including his tail, and he was as flat as two pancakes, and part of another one, and he couldn't even eat a toothpick.

Then, Uncle Wiggily and the boys fixed the hole in the tire, pumped it full of wind, and hurried on, and they had plenty of pumpkin left for pies, and they were soon at the squirrel's house, safe and sound, so that's the end of the story.

But on the next page, if the milk bottle doesn't roll down off the stoop and tickle the door-mat, I'll tell you about Uncle Wiggily and the pumpkin pie.

STORY VIII

UNCLE WIGGILY'S JACK-O'-LANTERN

"I REALLY think I must be traveling on to-day," said Uncle Wiggily, the nice old gentle-man rabbit, one bright morning when he had gone out to the Bushtail barn to see if there were any slivers sticking in the rubber tires of his automobile. "I have been here quite a while now, boys, and I want to pay a visit to some of my other friends," he added.

"Oh, please don't think of going!" begged Johnnie Bushtail, the boy squirrel.

"Please, can't you stay a little longer?" asked Billie, his brother. "Johnnie and I are going to make Jack-o'-lanterns to-night from the pumpkin you got us, and you may help if you like."

"Oh, that will be fine," said Uncle Wiggily. "I suppose I really must stay another night. But after that I shall have to be traveling along, for I have many more friends to visit, and only

to-day I had a letter from Jimmie Wibblewobble,
the duck boy, asking when I was coming to see
him."

"Well, never mind about that. Let's get to
work at making Jack-o'-lanterns now and not
wait for to-night," suggested Johnnie. "We'll
make three lanterns, one for Uncle Wiggily and
one for each of us."

So they sat down on benches out in the back
yard, where the pumpkin seeds wouldn't do any
harm, and they began to make the lanterns. And
this is how you do it. First you cut a little round
hole in the top of the pumpkin—the part where
the stem is, you know. And then you scoop out
the soft inside where all the seeds are, and you
can save the seeds to make more pumpkins grow
next year, if you like.

Then, after you have the inside all scraped
out clean, so that the shell is quite thin, you cut
out holes for the two eyes and a nose and a mouth,
and if you know how to do it you can cut make-
believe teeth in the Jack-o'-lantern's mouth.
If you can't do it yourselves, perhaps some of
the big folks will help you.

So that's how the squirrel boys and Uncle
Wiggily made their Jack-o'-lanterns, and when
they were all finished they put a lighted candle
inside and say! My goodness! It looked just

like a real person grinning at you, only, of course, it wasn't.

"Won't we have fun to-night!" exclaimed Johnnie as he finished his lantern.

"We certainly will!" said Billie, dancing a little jig.

"What are you going to do with your lantern, Uncle Wiggily?" asked Johnnie.

"Oh, I don't know," answered the old gentleman rabbit. "I may take it with me on my travels."

Well, after the three lanterns were made, there was still plenty of time before it would be dark, so Uncle Wiggily and the boys made some more lanterns. And along came Lulu and Alice and Jimmie Wibblewobble, the duck children, and as they had no Jack-o'-lanterns of their own, Johnnie gave Lulu one and Billie gave Alice one, and Uncle Wiggily gave Jimmie one, and my! you should have seen how pleased those duck children were! It was worth going across the street just to look at their smiling faces.

Well, pretty soon, after a while, not so very long, it was supper time, and there was pumpkin pie and carrot sandwiches and lettuce salad, and things like that for Uncle Wiggily, and nut cake and nut candy and nut sandwiches for the squirrels.

Uncle Wiggily was folding up his napkin, and he was just getting out of his chair to go in the parlor, and read the paper with Mr. Bushytail, when, all of a sudden, there came a knock on the front door.

"My goodness! I wonder who that can be?" exclaimed Mrs. Bushytail.

"I'll go see," spoke her husband, and when he went to the door there was kind old Mrs. Hop Toad on the mat, wiping her feet.

"Oh, is Uncle Wiggily Longears here?" asked Mrs. Toad. "If he is, tell him to come back to the rabbit house at once, for Sammie Littletail is very sick, and they can't get him to sleep, and the nurse thinks if he heard one of Uncle Wiggily's stories he would shut his eyes and rest."

"I'll come right away," said Uncle Wiggily, for he had gone to the front door, also, and had heard what Mrs. Hop Toad had said. "Wait until I get on my hat and coat and I'll crank up my automobile and go see Sammie," said the rabbit gentleman.

"I won't wait," said Mrs. Toad. "I'll hop on ahead, and tell them you're coming. Anyhow it gives me the toodle-oodles to ride in an auto."

So she hopped on ahead, and Uncle Wiggily

was soon ready to start off in his car. Just as he was going, Billie Bushytail cried out:

" Oh, Uncle Wiggily, take a Jack-o'-lantern with you and maybe Sammie will like that."

So the old gentleman rabbit took one of the pumpkin lanterns up on the seat with him, and away he went. And then, all at once, as he was going through a dark place in the woods in his auto, the wind suddenly blew out all his lanterns —all the oil lamps on the auto I mean, and right away after that a policeman dog cried out:

" Hey, there, Mr. Longears, you can't go on in your auto without a light, you know. It's against the law."

" I know it is," said Uncle Wiggily. " I'll light the lamps at once." But when he tried to do it he found there was no more oil in them.

" Oh, what shall I do? " he cried. " I'm in a hurry to get to Sammie Littletail, who is sick, but I can't go in the dark. Ah! I have it. The Jack-o'-lantern! I'll light the candle in that, and keep on going. Will that be all right, Mr. Policeman? "

" Sure it will," said the policeman dog, swing-ing his club, and wishing he was home in bed.

So Uncle Wiggily lighted the Jack-o'-lantern and it was real bright, and soon the old gentle-man rabbit was speeding on again. And, all of

a sudden out from the bushes jumped a burglar
fox.

" Hold on there! " he cried to Uncle Wiggily.
" I want all your money." And just then he
saw the big pumpkin Jack-o'-lantern, with its
staring eyes and big mouth and sharp teeth,
looking at him from the seat of the auto, and the
fox was so scared, thinking it was a giant going
to catch him, that he ran off in the woods how-
ling, and he didn't bother Uncle Wiggily a bit
more that night.

Then the old gentleman rabbit drove his auto
on toward Sammie's house, and he was soon there
and he told Sammie a funny story and gave him
the Jack-o'-lantern, and the little rabbit boy
was soon asleep, and in the morning he was all
better.

So that's what the Jack-o'-lantern did for
Uncle Wiggily and Sammie, and now if you
please you must go to bed, and on the page after
this, in case the basket of peaches doesn't fall
down the cellar stairs and break the furnace door
all to pieces, I'll tell you about Uncle Wiggily
and the lazy duck.

STORY IX

UNCLE WIGGILY AND THE LAZY DUCK

THE day after Uncle Wiggily had scared the bad burglar fox with the Jack-o'-lantern, the old rabbbit gentleman and Lulu and Alice and Jimmie Wibblewobble, the ducks, went for a little ride in the automobile.

For it was Saturday, you see, and there was no school. So they went along quite a distance over the hills and through the woods and fields, for Uncle Wiggily's auto was a sort of fairy machine and could go almost anywhere.

Pretty soon they came to a little house beside the road, and in the front yard was a nice pump, where you could get a drink of water.

"I am very thirsty," said Uncle Wiggily to Jimmie. "I wonder if we could get a drink here?"

"Oh, yes," said Lulu, as she looked to see if her hair ribbon was on straight; "a duck family lives here, and they will give you all the water you want."

Right after that, before Uncle Wiggily could get out of the auto to pump some water, there came waddling out of the duckhouse a duck boy, about as big as Jimmie.

"How do you do?" said Uncle Wiggily, politely to this duck boy. "May we get a drink of water here?"

"Oh—um—er—oo—I—guess—so," said the duck boy slowly, and he stretched out his wings and stretched out his legs and then he sat down on a bench in the front yard and nearly went to sleep.

"Why, I wonder what is the matter with him?" asked Uncle Wiggily. "Why does he act so strangely, and speak so slow?"

"I can tell you!" exclaimed Lulu, and she got down out of the auto and picked up a stone. "That duck boy is lazy, that's what's the matter with him. He never even wants to play. Why, at school he hardly ever knows his lessons."

"Oh, you surprise me!" said the old gentleman rabbit. "A lazy duck boy! I never heard of such a thing. Pray what is his name?"

"It's Fizzy-Whizzy," said Jimmie, who also knew the boy.

"Why, what a strange name!" exclaimed the rabbit gentleman. "Why do they call him that?"

" Because he is so fond of fizzy-izzy soda water," said Alice. " Oh, let's go along, Uncle Wiggily."

" No," said the rabbit gentleman, slowly, " if this is a lazy duck boy he should be cured. Laziness is worse than the measles or whooping cough, I think. And as I am very thirsty I want a drink. Then I will think of some plan to cure this boy duck of being lazy."

So Uncle Wiggily went close up to the boy duck and called out loud, right in his ear, so as to waken him:

" Will you please get me a cup so I may get a drink of water? "

" Hey? What's—that—you—said? " asked the lazy boy duck, slowly, stretching out his wings.

Uncle Wiggily told him over again, but that lazy chap just stretched his legs this time and said:

" Oh—I—am—too—tired—to—get—you — a —cup. You—had—better—go—in—the—house —and—get—it—for—yourself," and then he was going to sleep again.

But, all of a sudden, his mother, who worked very hard at washing and ironing, came to the door and said:

" Oh, dear! If Fizzy-Wizzy hasn't gone to

sleep again. Wake up at once, Fizzy, and get
me some wood for the fire! Quick."

"Oh—ma—I am—too—tired," said Fizzy-
Wizzy.   "I—will—do—it—to-morrow—um—
ah—er—boo—soo!" and he was asleep once
more.

"Oh, I never saw such a lazy boy in all my
life!" exclaimed the duck boy's mother, and she
was very much ashamed of him. "I don't know
what to do."

"Do you want me to make him better?" asked
Uncle Wiggily.

"Indeed I do, but I am afraid you can't," she
said.

"Yes I can," said Uncle Wiggily. "I'll come
back here this evening and I'll cure him. First
let me get a drink of water and then I'll think of
a way to do it." So the duck lady herself
brought out a cup so Uncle Wiggily and Lulu
and Alice and Jimmie could get a drink from the
pump, and all the while the lazy chap slept on.

"How are you going to cure him, Uncle Wiggily?" asked Jimmie when they were riding
along in the auto once more.

"I will show you," said the old gentleman
rabbit. "And you children must help me, for to
be lazy is a dreadful thing."

Well, that night, after dark, Uncle Wiggily

took a lantern, and some matches and some rubber balls and some beans and something else done up in a package, and he put all these things in his auto. Then he and the Wibblewobble children got in and they went to the house of the lazy boy duck.

" Is he in? " asked Uncle Wiggily of the boy's mamma.

" Yes," she said in a whisper.

" Well, when I throw a pebble against the kitchen window tell him to come out and see who's here," went on the rabbit gentleman. Then he opened the package and in it were four false faces, one of a fox, one of a wolf, one of a bear and one was of an alligator. And Uncle Wiggily put on the alligator false face, gave the bear one to Jimmie, the fox one to Alice and the wolf one to Lulu.

Then he gave Jimmie a handful of beans and he gave Alice a rubber ball filled with water to squirt and Lulu the same. They knew what to do with them. Then Uncle Wiggily built a fire and made some stones quite warm, not warm enough to burn one, but just warm enough.

These stones he put in front of the lazy duck boy's house and then he threw a pebble against the window.

"Go and see who is there," said the duck boy's mamma to him.

"I—don't—want—to," the lazy chap was just saying, but he suddenly became very curious and thought he would just take a peep out. And no sooner had he opened the door and stepped on the warm stones than he began to run down the yard, for he was afraid if he stood still he would be burned.

And then, as he ran, up popped Uncle Wiggily from behind the bushes, looking like an alligator with the false face on.

"Oh! Oh!" cried the lazy boy and he ran faster than ever.

Then up jumped Jimmie, looking like a bear with the false face on, and up popped Lulu looking like a wolf and Alice looking like a fox.

"Oh! Oh!" cried the lazy boy, and he ran faster than ever before in his life.

Then Alice and Lulu squirted water at him from their rubber balls.

"Oh! It's raining! It's raining!" cried the boy duck, and he ran faster than before.

Then Jimmie threw the beans at him and they rattled all over.

"Oh! It's snowing and hailing!" cried the lazy boy, and he ran faster than ever. And then Uncle Wiggily threw some hickory nuts at him, and that lazy duck ran still faster than he had ever run in his life before and ran back in the house.

"Oh, mother!" he cried, "I've had a terrible time," and he spoke very fast. "I'll never be lazy again."

"I'm glad of it," she said. "I guess Uncle Wiggily cured you."

And so the old gentleman rabbit had, for the duck boy was always ready to work after that. Then Lulu and Alice and Jimmie went home in the auto and went to bed, and that's where you must go soon.

And if the pussy cat doesn't slip in the molasses, and fall down the cellar steps, I'll tell you next about Uncle Wiggily helping Jimmie.

STORY X

UNCLE WIGGILY HELPS JIMMIE

OLD PERCIVAL, who used to be a circus dog, wasn't feeling very well. Some bad boys had tied a tin can to his tail, and had thrown stones at him and done other mean things. But Uncle Wiggily had come along and driven the boys away, and Percival had come home in the automobile of the old gentleman rabbit, and was given a nice warm place behind the kitchen stove, where he could lie down.

"But I don't feel a bit good," Percival said to Uncle Wiggily. "I don't know whether it was the tin can the boys tied to my tail, or the leaves they stuck on me, or the bone they put in my mouth or the molasses they used, but I don't feel at all well.

"Perhaps it is the epizootic," said Alice Wibblewobble, the duck girl, as she untied her green hair ribbon and put on a pink one.

"That may be it," said Percival, and he

blinked his two eyes slow and careful-like, so as
not to get any dust in them.

" Perhaps if I made you some dog-biscuit-soup
it would make you feel better," said Mrs. Wibblewobble. " I'll cook some right away."

So she did that and Percival ate it, but still
that night he didn't feel much better, and the
only trick he could do for the children was to
stand up on his tail, and make believe he was a
soldier. But he couldn't do that very long, and
then he had to crawl back to his bed behind the
stove.

" Poor Percival is getting old," said Mr. Wibblewobble. " He isn't the lively dog he used to be
when he showed Peetie and Jackie Bow Wow
how to do tricks in a circus parade.

" No, indeed," said Uncle Wiggily, and then
the old gentleman rabbit played blind man's bluff
with Lulu and Alice and Jimmie Wibblewobble
until it was time to go to bed.

Well, the next day poor old Percival wasn't
any better and when the duck children started
for school their mamma told them to stop on their
way home and tell Dr. Possum to come and give
Percival some medicine.

" We will," said Jimmie, and just then they
saw Uncle Wiggily putting some gasoline in his
automobile.

"Oh, dear! You're not going away, are you, Uncle Wiggily?" asked Lulu Wibblewobble as she picked up a stone and threw it even better than the lazy boy duck could have done.

"No," said the old gentleman rabbit, "I am just going for a little ride to see Grandfather Goosey Gander, but I will be back here when you come from school. Don't forget about telling Dr. Possum to come and see Percival."

So they said they wouldn't forget, and then the three duck children hurried on to school so they wouldn't be late, and Uncle Wiggily tickled the flinkum-flankum of his auto and away he went whizzing over the fields and through the woods.

Well, as it happened that day, Dr. Possum wasn't home, so all that Jimmie and his sisters could do was to leave word for him to come and see Percival as soon as the doctor got back.

"I'll send him right away, just as soon as he comes in," said Dr. Possum's wife. "Oh, I am so sorry for poor Percival."

Well, when Lulu and Alice and Jimmie got home from school Dr. Possum hadn't yet come to the duck house to see the sick dog, who was much worse. And Uncle Wiggily hadn't come back from his automobile ride, either.

"Oh, dear!" exclaimed Mrs. Wibblewobble.

"I don't know what to do! The doctor ought to come, and Uncle Wiggily ought to be here. Perhaps Uncle Wiggily has met with an accident and Dr. Possum had to attend to him first."

"Oh, I hope not, mamma," said Alice.

"I know what I can do," said Jimmie, the boy duck. "I can hurry back to Dr. Possum's house to see if he has come back yet. If he has I'll tell him to please hurry here."

"I think that would be a good idea," spoke Mrs. Wibble-wobble. "Go quickly, Jimmie, and here is a molasses cookie to eat on your way. Hurry back and bring the doctor with you if you can."

So Jimmie said he would, and off he started, eating the molasses cookie that his mamma had baked. He was thinking how good it was, and wishing it was larger when, all at once, he stepped on a sharp stone and hurt his foot so that he couldn't walk.

"Oh, dear!" cried Jimmie. "What shall I do? I can't go get Dr. Possum for Percival now."

Well, he was in great pain, and he was just wondering how he could send word to the doctor when, all at once, he saw a pony-horse in the field near by.

"The very thing!" exclaimed Jimmie. "That

is Munchie Trot, the pony boy, and he'll let me ride to the doctor on his back."

So Jimmie took a stick to use as a cane, and he managed to get right close up beside the pony-horse, who was eating grass.

" I'll surprise him," thought Jimmie. " I'll fly up on his back before he sees me."

So with his strong wings he flew up on the pony's back and he cried out:

" Surprise on you, Munchie! Please gallop and trot with me to Dr. Possum's so he can make Percival well."

And then a funny thing happened. All at once Jimmie noticed that he was on the back of a strange pony. It wasn't Munchie Trot at all! Jimmie had made a mistake. Think of that! And the worst of it was that when he flew so suddenly up on the pony's back Jimmie frightened him, and the next instant the pony jumped over the fence and began running down the road as fast as he could.

" Oh! Stop! Stop! " cried Jimmie. " I'll fall off! " The duck boy had to take hold of the pony's mane in his yellow bill, and he had to hold on so he wouldn't fall off. Faster and faster ran the pony, trying to get away from what was on his back, for he hadn't seen Jimmie fly up, and

he didn't know what it was.   Maybe he thought
it was a burglar fox, but I'm not sure.

Anyhow the pony went faster and faster, and
though Jimmie cried as hard as he could for him
to stop the pony wouldn't do it.   Jimmie was almost falling off, and he thought surely he would
be hurt, when, all of a sudden, down the road,
came Uncle Wiggily in his automobile.   He saw
what was the matter.

"Hold on, Jimmie!" cried the old gentleman
rabbit.   "Hold on, and I'll be up to you in a
minute.   Then you can fly into my auto and be
safe."

Well, the pony was going fast, but the auto
went faster, and it was soon up beside the little
galloping horsie.

"Now jump, Jimmie!" called Uncle Wiggily,
and the boy duck did so, landing safely in the
auto, and he wasn't hurt a bit.

Then the pony galloped on until he looked
back and saw it had only been a duck on his
back and then he was ashamed for having run
away, and he stopped and said he was sorry, so
Jimmie forgave him.

"Quick, we must go for Dr. Possum for Old
Dog Percival," said Jimmie, and he told Uncle
Wiggily how the doctor hadn't yet come.   Then
Uncle Wiggily told how he accidentally got a

hole in one of his big rubber tires or he would have been home sooner.

"But it's a good thing I happened to come along to help you," he said to Jimmie, and Jimmie thought so too. Then they went for Dr. Possum, who had just come home, and they took him to Percival in the auto, and Dr. Possum soon made Percival all well, and I'm glad of it. Then the doctor cured Jimmie's sore foot, and everybody was happy, and I hope you are.

And next, if the dried leaves don't blow in my window and scare the wallpaper so that it falls off, I'll tell you about Uncle Wiggily helping Alice.

STORY XI

ONE day the postman bird flew down out of
the sky and stopped in front of the Wibblewobble duck house. Uncle Wiggily Longears,
the old gentleman rabbit, was out in front, cleaning some mud off his auto, for he had run it very
fast into a puddle of water the day he saved Jimmie off the pony's back.

" Does anybody named Alice Wibblewobble
live here? " asked the postman bird as he looked
in his bag of letters.

" Yes, Alice lives here," said Uncle Wiggily.

" And does Lulu Wibblewobble? "

" Yes, of course."

" And Jimmie, too? "

" Certainly," said the old gentleman rabbit.

" Then this is the right house," said the postman bird as he blew his whistle, like a canary,
" and here is a letter for each of them."

So he handed Uncle Wiggily three letters and
then he flew up into the air again, as fast as he
could go, to deliver the rest of the mail.

"Hum! I wonder who can be writing to Lulu and Alice and Jimmie?" said Uncle Wiggily, as he looked at the letters. "Well, I'll take them in the house. They look to me like party invitations; and I wonder why I didn't get one? But I suppose the young folks don't want an old rheumatic uncle around any more. Ah, well, I'm getting old—getting old," and he went slowly into the house, feeling a bit sad.

"Here are some letters for you, children," he called to Lulu and Alice and Jimmie. "The bird postman just brought them."

"Oh, fine!" cried the children, and they opened them all at once with their strong yellow bills.

"Goodie!" cried Lulu as she read hers. "Jennie Chipmunk is going to have a party, and I'm invited."

"So am I," cried Alice.

"And I," added Jimmie.

"I thought they were party invitations," said Uncle Wiggily, sort of sad and thoughtful-like. "When is it?"

"To-night," said Lulu.

"Then we must hurry and get ready," said Alice. "I must iron out some of my hair ribbons so they will be nice and fresh."

"Oh, that's just like you girls," cried Jimmie.

"You have to primp and fuss. I can be ready in no time, just by washing my face."

"Oh!" cried Lulu and Alice together. "Make him put on a clean collar, anyhow, mamma."

"Yes, I'll do that," agreed Jimmie.

Well, pretty soon they were all getting ready to go to the party, and Uncle Wiggily went back to finish cleaning his auto and he was wishing he could go. But you just wait and see what happens.

Pretty soon it became night and then it was time for the party. Lulu and Jimmie were all ready, but it took Alice such a long time to get her hair fixed the way she wanted it, and to get just the kind of hair ribbon that suited her, that she wasn't ready. You see, she had so many kinds of hair ribbons and she kept them all in a box, and really she didn't know just which one to take. First she picked out a red one, and she didn't like that, and then she picked out a blue one, and she didn't like that, and then she picked up a pink one, and then a green, and then a brown, and finally a skilligimink colored one, but none suited her.

"Hurry, Alice," called Lulu, "or you'll be late."

"Oh, you can go on ahead and I'll catch up to you and Jimmie," said Alice, trying another hair ribbon.

"All right," they answered, and they started off. Mr. and Mrs. Wibblewbobble had gone across the street to pay a little visit to Mr. and Mrs. Duckling, and so Uncle Wiggily and Alice were all alone in the house.

"You had better hurry, Alice," said the old gentleman rabbit as he was reading the evening paper.

"Oh, I don't know what to do!" she cried. "I can't decide which hair ribbon to wear."

"Wear them all," called Uncle Wiggily with a laugh, but, of course, Alice couldn't do that, and she was in despair, which means that she didn't know what to do.

She laid all the ribbons back in the box, and she was just going to shut her eyes, and pick out the first one she could reach, and wear that whether she liked it or not, for she didn't want to be late to the party. And then, all of a sudden, in through the open window of her room the old skillery-scalery alligator put his long nose and he cried:

"Hair ribbons! I must have hair ribbons! Give me hair ribbons!"

And then what do you think he did?" Why, he grabbed up the whole box full of Alice's lovely hair ribbons, and before she could say " scootum-scattum," if she had wanted to, that skillery scalery alligator ran away with them in his mouth, taking his double-jointed tail with him.

"Oh!" cried Alice. "Oh! Oh!" and she almost lost her breath, she was so surprised.

"What is it?" cried Uncle Wiggily, running up to her room.

"The alligator! He has taken my hair ribbons. Quick, run after him, dear Uncle Wiggily!"

"I will!" exclaimed the brave old gentleman rabbit and out of the house he hurried, but the 'gator with the double-jointed tail had completely gone, and the rabbit gentleman couldn't catch him.

"Oh, what ever shall I do?" cried Alice, when Uncle Wiggily came back. "I have no hair ribbon, and I can't go to the party!"

Well, Uncle Wiggily thought for a moment. He didn't tell Alice that she should have hurried more and worn a pink ribbon, and then the accident wouldn't have happened. No, he didn't say anything like that; but he said:

"I can help you, Alice. Down in the yard is some long grass, green, with white stripes in it. They call it ribbon grass. I will get some for a hair ribbon for you."

"Oh, thank you, so much!" said Alice. So Uncle Wiggily quickly went down, pulled some

of the ribbon grass and helped Alice tie it in her
feathers. And she looked too cute for anything,
really she did.

"Now, quick, run and catch up to Jimmie and
Lulu, and go to the party and have a good time,"
said Uncle Wiggily, and Alice did. And what
do you think? A little while after that up to the
duck-house drove Sammie Littletail in a pony
cart.

"Oh, Uncle Wiggily!" cried Sammie, "Jennie Chipmunk was so flustrated about her party
that she forgot to send you an invitation. But
she wants you very much, so I've come to take
you to it. Come along with me!"

Then Uncle Wiggily was very glad, for he
liked parties as much as you do, and he jumped
into the cart with Sammie and they went to the
party and had a lovely time. And the next day
Uncle Wiggily went out in his auto, and he made
the alligator give back all of Alice's hair ribbons,
and none of them was lost or soiled the least bit,
I'm glad to say.

Now, no more at present, if you please, but
if the picture book doesn't read about the sand-
man and go to sleep on the front porch, I'll tell
you next about Uncle Wiggily and the doll
doctor.

STORY XII

UNCLE WIGGILY AND THE DOLL DOCTOR

"Now, I wonder where I will go to-day?"
said Uncle Wiggily, the old gentleman rabbit to
himself, as he went along, in his automobile, turning around the corner by an old black stump-
house, where lived a nice owl school teacher lady.
"I wonder where I had better go? I have it!
I'll call on Grandfather Goosey Gander and play
a game of Scotch checkers!" and off he went.

It was generally that way with Uncle Wiggily. He would start off pretending he had no
place in particular to go, but he would generally
end up at Grandpa Goosey's house.

There the old rabbit gentleman and the old
duck gentleman would sit and play Scotch
checkers and eat molasses cookies with cabbage
seeds on top, and they would talk of the days
when they were young, and could play ball and
go skating, and do all of those things.

But this time Uncle Wiggily never got to

Grandfather Goosey's house As he was going
along in the woods, all of a sudden he came to a
little house that stood under a Christmas tree,
and on this house was a sign reading:

DR. MONKEY DOODLE. SICK DOLLS
MADE WELL.

"Ha! That is rather strange!" exclaimed
Uncle Wiggily. "I never knew there was a doll
doctor here. He must have moved in only lately.
I must look into this!"

So the rabbit gentleman went up to the little
house, and, as he came nearer he heard some one
inside exclaiming:

"Oh, I'll never get through to-day, I know I
won't! Oh, the trouble I'm in! Oh, if I only
had some one to help me!"

"My! What is that!" cried Uncle Wiggily,
stopping short. "Perhaps I am making a mistake. That may be a trap! No, it doesn't look
like a trap," he went on, as he peered all about
the little house and saw nothing dangerous.

Then the voice cried again:

"Oh, I am in such trouble! Will no one help
me?"

Now Uncle Wiggily was always on the look-
out to help his animal friends, but he did not
know who this one could be.

" Still," said the rabbit gentleman to himself,
" he is in trouble. Maybe a mosquito has bitten
him. I'm going to see."

So Uncle Wiggily marched bravely up to the
little house under the Christmas tree, and
knocked on the door.

" Come in! " cried a voice. " But if you're a
little animal girl, with a sick doll, or one that
needs mending, you might as well go away and
come back again. I'm head-over heels in work,
and I'll never get through. In fact I can't work
at all. Oh, such trouble as I am in! "

" Well, maybe I can help you," said Uncle
Wiggily. " At any rate I have no doll that needs
mending."

So into the little house he went, and what a
queer sight he saw! There was Dr. Monkey
Doodle, sitting on the floor of his shop, and scattered all about him were dolls—dolls—dolls!

All sorts of dolls—but not a good, whole, well
doll in the lot. Some dolls had lost their wigs,
some had swallowed their eyes, others had lost a
leg, or both arms, or a foot.

One poor doll had lost all her sawdust, and she
was as flat as a pancake. Another had dropped
one of her shoe button eyes, and a new eye needed
to be sewed in. One doll had stiff joints, which
needed oiling, while another, who used to talk in

a little phonograph voice, had caught such a cold
that she could not speak or even whisper.

"My, what sort of a place is this?" asked
Uncle Wiggily, in surprise.

"It is the doll hospital," said Dr. Monkey
Doodle. "Think of it! All these dolls to fix before night, and I can't touch a one of them!"

"Why must all the dolls be fixed to-night?"
the rabbit gentleman wanted to know.

"Because they are going to a party," ex-
plained Dr. Monkey Doodle. "Susie Littletail,
the rabbit is giving a party for all the little animal
girls, and every one is going to bring her doll.
But all the dolls were ill, or else were broken, and
the animal children brought them all to me at
once, so that I am fairly overwhelmed with work,
if you will kindly permit me to say so," remarked the monkey doctor.

"Of course, I'll let you say so," said Uncle
Wiggily. "But, if you will kindly pardon me,
why don't you get up and work, instead of sitting
in the middle of the floor, feeling sorry for yourself?"

"True! Why do I not?" asked the monkey
doctor. "Well, to be perfectly plain, I am stuck
here so fast that I can't move. One of the dolls,
I think it was Cora Ann Multiplicationtable, upset the pot of glue on the floor. I came in hur-

riedly, and, not seeing the puddle of glue, I slipped in it. I fell down, I sat right in the glue, and now I am stuck so fast that I can't get up.

"So you see that's why I can't work on the broken dolls. I can't move! And oh, what a time there'll be when all those animal girls come for their dolls and find they're not done. Oh, what a time I'll have!"

And the monkey doctor tried to pull himself up from the glue on the floor, but he could not— he was stuck fast.

"Oh, dear!" he cried.

"Now don't worry!" spoke Uncle Wiggily kindly. "I think I can help you."

"Oh, can you!" cried Dr. Monkey Doodle. "And will you?"

"I certainly will," said Uncle Wiggily, tying his ears in a bowknot so they would not get tangled in the glue.

"But how can you help me?" asked the monkey doctor.

"In the first place," went on the rabbit gentleman. "I will pour some warm water all around you on the glue. That will soften it, and by-and-by you can get up. And while we are waiting for that you shall tell me how to cure the sick dolls and how to mend the broken ones and I'll do the best I can."

"Fine!" cried Dr. Monkey Doodle, feeling happier now.

So Uncle Wiggily poured some warm water on the glue that held the poor monkey fast, taking care not to have the water too hot. Then Uncle Wiggily said:

"Now, we'll begin on the sick dolls. Who's first?"

"Take Sallie Jane Ticklefeather," said the monkey. "She needs some mucilage pills to keep her hair from sticking up so straight. She belongs to a little girl named Rosalind."

So Uncle Wiggily gave Sallie Jane Ticklefeather some mucilage pills. Then he gave another doll some sawdust tea and a third one some shoe-button pudding—this was the doll who only had one eye—and soon she was all cured and had two eyes.

And then such a busy time as Uncle Wiggily had! He hopped about that little hospital, sewing arms and legs and feet on the dolls that had lost theirs. He oiled up all the stiff joints with olive oil, and one doll, whose eyes had fallen back in her head, Uncle Wiggily fixed as nicely as you please. Only by mistake he got in one brown eye and one blue one, but that didn't matter much. In fact, it made the doll all the more stylish.

" Oh, but there are a lot more dolls to fix! "
cried the monkey doctor.

" Never mind," said Uncle Wiggily. " You
will soon be loose from the glue, and you can help
me! "

" Oh, I wish I were loose now! " cried the
monkey.

He gave himself a tremendous tug and a pull,
Uncle Wiggily helping him, and up he came.
Then how he flew about that hospital, fixing the
dolls ready for the party.

" Hark! " suddenly called Uncle Wiggily.

" It's the girl animals coming for their dolls,"
said the monkey. " Oh, work fast! Work fast! "

Outside the doll hospital Susie Littletail, the
rabbit girl, and Alice and Lulu Wibblewobble,
the duck girls, and all their friends were calling:

" Are our dolls mended? Are they ready for
us? "

" Not yet, but soon," answered Uncle Wiggily,
and then he and the monkey worked so fast!
Dolls that had lost their heads had new ones put
on. The doll that had spilled all her sawdust
was filled up again, plump and fat. One boy
soldier doll, who had lost his gun was given a new
one, and a sword also. And the phonograph doll
was fixed so that she could sing as well as talk.

"But it is almost time for the party!" cried
Susie Littletail.

"Just a minute!" called Uncle Wiggily.
"There is one more doll to fix." Then he
quickly painted some red cheeks on a poor little
pale doll, who had had the measles, and in a
moment she was as bright and rosy again as a red
apple. Then all the dolls were fixed, and the
girl animals took them to a party and had a fine
time.

"Hurray for Uncle Wiggily!" cried Susie
Littletail, and all the others said the same thing.

"He certainly was kind to me," spoke Dr.
Monkey Doodle, as he cleaned the glue up off the
floor. And that's all there is to this story, but in
the next one, if the goldfish doesn't bite a hole
in his globe and let all the molasses run over the
tablecloth, I'll tell you about Uncle Wiggily and
the flowers.

STORY XIII

UNCLE WIGGILY AND THE FLOWERS

ONE Saturday, when there was no school, Charley Chick was playing soldier in the chicken coop, and beating the drum that Uncle Wiggily had given him, for Christmas.

And Arabella, who was Charley's sister, was playing with her talking doll. The little chicken girl was teaching the doll to recite that piece about " Once a trap was baited, with a piece of cheese." But the doll couldn't seem to get the verses right. She would say it something like this:

" Once a trap was baited,
  With a twinkling star.
'Twas Christmas eve and Santa Claus
  Was coming from afar.

" A little drop of water,
  Was in Jack Horner's pie
When Mary lost her little lamb
  Old Mother Goose did cry."

93

"Oh, you'll never get that right!" exclaimed Arabella. "Uncle Wiggily, can't you make my talking doll learn to speak pieces right? She gets them all mixed up."

"I'll try," said the old gentleman rabbit, and he was just telling the doll how to recite a poem about little monkey-jack upon a stick of candy, and every time he took a bite it tasted fine and dandy. Well, the doll had learned one verse, when, all at once, there came a knock on the door, and there stood a telegraph messenger boy, with a telegram for Uncle Wiggily.

"Oh, something has happened!" exclaimed Mrs. Chick. "I am so nervous whenever telegrams come."

"Wait until I read it," said the old gentleman rabbit, and when he had read it he said: "It is from Aunt Lettie, the old lady goat. She has the epizootic very badly, from having eaten some bill-board pictures of a snowstorm, which made her catch cold, and she wants to know if I can't come over to see her, and tell Dr. Possum to bring her some medicine. Of course I will. I'll start off at once."

So Uncle Wiggily started off, in his automobile, and on his way to see the old lady goat he stopped at the doctor's house, and Dr. Possum promised to come as soon as he could, and cure the old lady goat.

"Then I'll go on ahead," spoke Uncle Wiggily, "and tell her you are coming." So he hurried on, with his long ears flapping to and fro, and he hadn't gone very far before he came to a shop where a man had flowers to sell—roses and violets and pinks and all lovely blossoms like that.

"The very thing!" exclaimed Uncle Wiggily, as he saw the pretty posies. "Sick persons like flowers, and I'll take some to Aunt Lettie. They may cheer her up." So he bought a large bouquet and kept on toward the lady goat's house.

Well, he hadn't gone very far before, all at once, as he was going around the corner by the prickly briar bush, that had berries on it in the summer time, all at once, I say, out jumped a big black bear.

At first Uncle Wiggily thought it was a good bear, and he stopped the auto to shake paws with him. But, all at once, he saw that it was a bad bear, whom he had never seen before.

"Oh, my!" exclaimed Uncle Wiggily, surprised-like. "I—I guess I have made a mistake. I don't know you. I beg your pardon."

"You don't need to do that," growled the bear. "You'll soon know me well enough. You and I are going to be very well acquainted soon. You

come with me," and with that he grabbed hold of
the old gentleman rabbit and marched off with
him, pulling him right out of the auto.

"Where are you taking me?" asked Uncle
Wiggily, trying to be brave, and not shiver or
shake.

"To my den," answered the bear in a grillery-
growlery voice. "I haven't had my Christmas
or New Year's dinner yet, and here it is the middle of January. Bur-r-r-r-r-r-r! Wow!"

"Oh, what a savage bear," exclaimed Uncle
Wiggily. "What makes you so cross?"

"Just look at my feet and you'll see why,"
answered the bear, and Uncle Wiggily looked,
and as true as I'm telling you, there were a whole
lot of walnut shells fast on the bear's feet.
"That's enough to make any one cross," said the
bear. "I stepped in these shells that some one
threw out of their window after Christmas, and
they stuck on so tight that I can't get them off.
Talk about corns! These are worse than any
corns. I have to walk on my tiptoes all the while,
and I'm so cross that I could eat a hot cross bun
and never know it. Bur-r-r-r-r! Wow! Woof!"

"Oh, my!" exclaimed Uncle Wiggily.
"Then I guess it's all up with me, and he felt
quite sad-like.

"You may well say that!" growled the bear.

"Come along!" and he almost pulled Uncle
Wiggily head over paws. "What have you in
that paper?" asked the bear, as he saw the bag of
flowers in Uncle Wiggily's paw.

"Some blossoms for poor sick Aunt Lettie!"
answered the rabbit gentleman. "Poor, sick
Aunt Lettie——"

"Bur-r-r-r-r! Wow! Woof! Bah! Don't
talk to me about sick goats!" growled the bear.
"I'm sicker than any goat of these walnut shells
on my feet. Bur-r-r-r-r! Wow! Woof!

And then Uncle Wiggily thought of something. Gently opening the paper he took out one
nice, big, sweet-smelling rose and handed it to
the bear, saying nothing.

"Bur-r-r-r-r! Wow! What's this?" growled
the bear, and before he knew what he was doing
he had taken the rose in his big paws. And then,
before he knew, the next thing, he was smelling
of it.

And, as he smelled the sweet perfume, he
seemed to think he was in the summer fields, all
covered with flowers, and as he looked at the rose
it seemed to remind him of the time when he was
a little bear, and wasn't bad, and didn't say such
things as "Bur-r-r-r-r!" "Wow!" And then
once more he smelled of the perfume in the flower,

and he seemed to forget the pain of the walnut shells on his feet.

"Oh, Uncle Wiggily!" exclaimed the bear, and tears came into his blinkery-inkery eyes, and rolled down his black nose. "I'm sorry I was bad to you. This flower is so lovely that it makes me want to be good. Run along, now, before I change my mind and get bad again."

"First let me help you take those walnut shells off your paws," said the rabbit gentleman, and he did so, prying them off with a stick, and then the bear felt ever so much better and he hurried to his den, still smelling the beautiful rose. So you see flowers are sometimes good, even for bears.

Then Uncle Wiggily hurried on to Aunt Lettie's house with the rest of the bouquet, and when she saw it she was quite some better, and when Dr. Possum gave her some medicine she was all better, and she thought Uncle Wiggily was very brave to do as he had done to the bear.

And on the next page, in case the eggbeater doesn't hit the rolling pin and make the potato masher fall down in the ice cream cone, I'll tell you about Uncle Wiggily and Susie's doll.

STORY XIV

UNCLE WIGGILY AND SUSIE'S DOLL

"WELL, I see you are going out for another ride in your auto," remarked Mrs. Bow Wow, the puppy dog lady, to Uncle Wiggily, one morning, after Peetie and Jackie had gone to school. "Where are you bound for now?"

"Oh, no place in particular," he said. "I just thought I would take a ride for my health."

You see the rabbit gentleman had come to pay the dog family a visit.

"I should think you'd stay in when it snows," went on the doggie lady. "You seem always to be out in a snowstorm," for it was snowing quite hard just then.

"I love the snow," said the old gentleman rabbit. "I like cold weather, for then my thick fur coat keeps me much warmer than in the summer time. And I like the snow—I like to see it come down, and feel it blow in my face and make my auto go through the drifts."

"Well, be careful you don't get stuck in any

drifts and freeze fast," said Mrs. Bow Wow, as she began washing the breakfast dishes.

" I'll try not to," promised Uncle Wiggily, and then he put some oil on his auto, and gave it a drink of warm water (for autos get thirsty sometimes), and away the old gentleman rabbit rode through the snowstorm.

" I guess I'll go call on Aunt Lettie, the old lady goat, to-day," he thought as he went through a big snowdrift, scattering the snow on both sides like an electric-car snow plow. " I haven't seen Aunt Lettie in some time, and she may be ill again." For this was some time after Uncle Wiggily had brought her the flowers.

Well, pretty soon he was at the old lady goat's house, and, surely enough she had been ill again. She had eaten some red paper, off the outside of a tomato can, one day right after Christmas, and the paper didn't have the right kind of stick-umpaste on it, so Aunt Lettie was taken ill on that account.

" But I'm much better now," she said to Uncle Wiggily, " and I'm real glad you called. Come in and I'll give you a hot cup of old newspaper tea."

" Um, I don't know as I care for that," said the old gentleman rabbit, making his nose twinkle like a star on a frosty night.

"Oh, I'm surprised to hear you say that,"
spoke Aunt Lettie, sorrowful-like. " Newspaper
tea is very good, especially with cream-stickum-
mucilage in it. But never mind, I'll give you
some carrot tea," and she did, and she and Uncle
Wiggily sat and talked about old times, and the
fun Nannie and Billie Goat used to have, until
it was time for the old gentleman rabbit to go
back home.

School was out as he went along in his auto.
He could tell that because he met so many of the
animal children. And he gave Peetie and Jackie
Bow Wow and Johnnie and Billie Bushtail a
ride toward home. But before they got there,
all of a sudden, as the four animal children were
in the auto, and Uncle Wiggily was making it go
through a snowdrift, all of a sudden, I say the
old gentleman rabbit turned around a corner,
and there was Susie Littletail, the little rabbit
girl, standing in front of a big heap of snow.

And she was crying very hard, her tears falling
down, and making little holes in the snow, and she
was poking into the drift with a long stick.

"Why, Susie!" asked Uncle Wiggily, " whatever is the matter?"

"Oh, my doll! My lovely, big, new Christmas
doll!" cried Susie. " I had her to school with me,
for we are learning to sew in our class, and I was

making my dollie a new dress, and—and—" and
then poor Susie cried so hard that she couldn't
talk.

"Don't tell me some one took your doll away
from you!" exclaimed Uncle Wiggily.

"If they did I'll go after them and get it back
for you!" cried Jackie Bow Wow.

"So will I!" said Peetie and Billie and
Johnnie.

"No, it isn't that," spoke the little rabbit girl.
"But as I was walking along, with my dollie in
my arms, all of a sudden she slipped out, fell
into this big snowbank, and I can't find her!
She's all covered up. Boo hoo! Hoo boo!"

"Oh, don't take on so," said Uncle Wiggily
kindly. "We will all help you hunt for your
dollie; won't we, boys?"

"Sure!" cried Peetie and Jackie and Billie
and Johnnie.

So they all got sticks and poked in the snow
bank, Uncle Wiggily poking harder than anybody, but it was of no use. They couldn't seem
to find that lost doll.

"She must be very deep under the snow!"
said Uncle Wiggily.

"Oh, I'll never see her again!" cried Susie.
"My big, beautiful Christmas doll. Boo-hoo!
Hoo-boo!"

" You can get her when the snow melts," spoke
Peetie Bow Wow, as he scratched away at the
drift with his paws.

" Yes, but then the wax will be all melted off
her face, and she won't look like anything,"
murmured Susie, sad-like.

" Wait; I have a plan," said Uncle Wiggily.
" There is a fan, like an electric one, in the front
part of my auto to keep the water cool. I'll make
that fan blow the snow away and we'll get your
doll."

So he tried that, making the fan whizz around
like a boy's top, but, though it blew some snow
away, the doll couldn't be found.

" Oh, I'll never see my big, beautiful doll
again! " cried Susie.

" Oh, whatever is the matter? " asked a voice,
and, turning around, they all saw the big, black,
woolly bear standing there. At first the animal
children were frightened until Uncle Wiggily
said:

" Oh, that bear won't hurt us. I once helped
him get some walnut shells off his paws, so he is
a friend of mine."

" Of course I am," said the bear. " What is
the trouble? " Then they told him about Susie's
doll being under the drift, and the bear went on:
" Don't worry about that. My paws are just

made for digging in the snow. I'll have that doll for you in a jiffy, which is very quick." So with his paws he began digging in the snow.

My! how he did make the snow fly, and he blew it away with his strong breath. Faster and faster flew the snow, and in about a minute it was all scraped away, and there was Susie's doll safe and sound. And she was sleeping with her eyes shut.

"Oh, you darling!" Susie cried, clasping the doll in her arms.

"Did you mean me?" asked the bear, laughing.

"Yes, I guess I did!" said Susie, also laughing, and she gave the bear a nice little kiss on the end of his black nose.

Then everybody was happy and the bear went back to his den and Uncle Wiggily took the children and the doll home, and that's all I can tell you now, if you please.

But, if the rocking horse doesn't run away and upset the milk pitcher down in the salt cellar and scare the furnace so that it goes out, I'll tell you in the story after this one, about Uncle Wiggily on roller skates.

STORY XV

UNCLE WIGGILY ON ROLLER SKATES

"WELL, where are you going this morning?" asked Jimmie Wibblewobble, the duck boy, as he looked out of the front door of his house, and saw Uncle Wiggily, the old gentleman rabbit, putting some gasoline in his automobile.

"Oh, I am going to take a little ride out in the country," said Uncle Wiggily. "I am going to see if I can find an adventure. Nothing has happened since we found Susie's doll. I must have excitement. It keeps me from thinking about my rheumatism. So I am going to look for an adventure, Jimmie."

"I wish I could come," said the little duck boy.

"I wish you could too," said his uncle. "But you must go to school. Some Saturday I'll take you with me, and we may find an adventure for each of us."

"And for us girls, too?" asked Lulu and Alice as they came out, all ready to go to school.

Alice had just finished tying her sky-yellow-green hair ribbon into two lovely bow knots.

"Yes, for you duck girls, too," said Uncle Wiggily. "But I will be back here when you come from school, and if anything happens to me I'll tell you all about it."

So he kept on putting gasoline in his automobile until he had the tinkerum-tankerum full, and then he tickled the hickory-dickory-dock with a mucilage brush, and he was all ready to start off and look for an adventure.

So Lulu and Alice and Jimmie went on to school, and Uncle Wiggily rode along over the fields and through the woods and up hill and down hill.

Pretty soon, as he was riding along, he heard a funny little noise in the bushes. It was a sad, little, squeaking sort of noise and at first the old gentleman rabbit thought it was made by something on his automobile that needed oiling. Then he looked over the side and there, sitting under an old cabbage leaf, was a little mousie girl, and it was she who was crying.

"Oh, ho!" exclaimed Uncle Wiggily, "is that you, Squeaky-eaky?" for he thought it might be the little cousin-mouse who lived with Jollie and Jillie Longtail, as I have told you in other stories.

" No, I am not Squeaky-eaky," said the little mouse girl, " but I am cold and hungry and I don't know what to do or where to go. Oh, dear! Boo-hoo! "

" Never mind," said Uncle Wiggily kindly. " I will take you in my auto, and I'll bring you to the house where the Longtail children live, and they'll take care of you."

" Oh, goody! " cried the little girl mouse. " Thank you so much. Now I am happy." So Uncle Wiggily took her in the nice, warm automobile.

Then he twisted the noodleum-noddleum until it sneezed, and away the auto went through the woods again. And, all of a sudden, just as Uncle Wiggily came to a big black stump, out jumped the burglar bear with roller skates on his paws.

" Hold on there! " the bear cried to the old gentleman rabbit, and he poked a stick in the auto wheels, so they couldn't go around any more. " Hold on, if you please, Mr. Rabbit. I want you."

" What for? " asked Uncle Wiggily.

" I want you to come to supper," said the burglar bear.

" Your supper or my supper? " asked Uncle Wiggily, politely.

" My supper, of course," said the burglar bear.

"I am going to have rabbit pot-pie to-night, **and** you are going to be both the rabbit and the **pie.** Come, now, get out of that auto. I want to **ride** in it before I bite you."

Well, of course, Uncle Wiggily felt pretty badly, but there was no help for it. He had to get out, and then the burglar bear, taking off his roller skates, got up into the automobile.

"Oh, what nice soft cushions!" exclaimed the bear as he sank down on them. Then he took hold of the turnip steering wheel in his claws and twisted it. "I shall have lots of fun riding in this auto, after I gobble you up," said the bear, looking at the rabbit with his blinky eyes. "I must learn to run it. I think I'll take a little ride before I have my supper. But don't you dare run away, for I can catch you."

Then, to make sure Uncle Wiggily couldn't get away, the bear took the old rabbit gentleman's crutch away from him and Uncle Wiggily's rheumatism was so severe, which means painful, that he couldn't walk a step without his crutch. So there was no use for him to try to run away.

Well, the bear knew how to run the auto, it seems, and he started to take a little ride in it. Uncle Wiggily felt pretty sad because he **was** going to be gobbled up and lose his auto at the same time.

All at once, when the bear in the auto was some distance off in the woods, Uncle Wiggily heard a little voice speaking to him.

"Hey, Uncle Wiggily," the voice said, "I know how you can get the best of that bear?"

"How?" asked Uncle Wiggily, eagerly.

"Here are his roller skates," said the voice, and it was the little mousie girl who was speaking. She had quietly jumped out of the auto. "Put on his roller skates," said the mousie, "and skate down the hill until you see a policeman dog. Then tell the policeman dog to come and arrest the bear. He'll do it, and then you'll get your auto back. You can go on roller skates even if you have rheumatism, can't you?"

"I guess so," said the rabbit. "I'll try." So he put on the skates while the burglar bear was making the auto go around in a circle in the woods, and that bear was having a good time. All at once Uncle Wiggily skated away. First he went slowly, and then he went faster and faster until he was just whizzing along. And then, at the foot of the hill, he found the policeman dog.

"Oh, please come and arrest the burglar bear for me?" begged Uncle Wiggily.

"To be sure I will," said the policeman dog. So he put on his roller skates, and skated back with Uncle Wiggily to where the bear was still in the auto. The policeman dog hid behind a stump. The bear stopped the auto in front of Uncle Wiggily and got out.

"Well," said the burglar bear, smacking his lips, "I guess it's supper time now. I'm going to eat you. Come on and be my pot-pie!" And he made a grab for the old gentleman rabbit.

"Oh, you will; will you?" suddenly cried the policeman dog, drawing his club, and jumping from behind the stump. "Well, I guess you won't eat my good friend, Uncle Wiggily. I guess not!" and with that the policeman dog tickled the bear so on his nose that he sneezed, and ran off through the woods taking his stubby little tail with him, but leaving behind his roller skates.

"Oh, I'm ever so much obliged to you, Policeman Dog," said the old gentleman rabbit, as he took off the bear's skates. "You saved my life. I'll take these skates home to Jimmie. They will fit him when he grows bigger."

"That is a good idea," said the dog, "and if I ever catch that bear again I will put him in the beehive jail and make him crack hickory nuts with his teeth."

Then Uncle Wiggily went home, and took the little mousie girl with him, and he told the duck children about his adventure with the bear, just as I have told you. So now it's bedtime, if you please, and I can't tell you any more.

But if the man who cleans our yard doesn't take my overcoat for an ash can and put the dried leaves in it, I'll tell you next about Uncle Wiggily and the clothes wringer.

STORY XVI

UNCLE WIGGILY AND THE CLOTHES WRINGER

One day Jackie and Peetie Bow Wow, the little puppy dog boys, came running over to Uncle Wiggily's hollow stump-house. It was after school, from which they had just come, and they rushed up the front steps, barking like anything, and calling out:

"Where's Uncle Wiggily? Where is he?"

"We want to see him in a hurry!" barked Peetie.

"Yes, immediately," went on Jackie. He had heard the teacher that day in school use the word, immediately, to tell a bad bumble bee to take his seat and stop trying to sting Lulu Wibblewobble. Immediately means right off quick, without waiting, you know.

"Hoity-toity!" cried Nurse Jane Fuzzy-Wuzzy, the muskrat housekeeper. "What is the trouble?"

"We must see Uncle Wiggily immediately!"

112

barked Peetie again, trying to stand on one ear.
But he could not make it stiff enough, so he fell
down, and bumped into Jackie, and they both
tumbled down the steps, making a great racket.

"There, there! You must be more quiet,"
cautioned Nurse Jane. "Uncle Wiggily just
came back from his auto ride for his health, and is
taking a nap. You must not wake him up.
What do you want to see him about that is so im-
portant?"

"Oh, we'll wait until he wakes up," said
Jackie, as he sat down on the porch.

"Ha! Who wants me?" suddenly exclaimed
a voice a little later, and out came Uncle Wiggily himself.

"We do!" cried Jackie. "Oh, Uncle Wiggily!"

"We're going to work!" added Peetie, unable
to keep still any longer.

"What! You don't mean to say you're going
to leave school and go to work?" asked Uncle
Wiggily.

"No, we're not going to leave school," exclaimed Peetie. "We are going to work after
school. Jackie is going to deliver newspapers."

"And I'm going to get ten cents a week for it,"
said Jackie proudly, but not too proud.

"And I'm going to help at the clothes wringer

for the circus elephant," exclaimed Peetie.

"Help at the wringer for the elephant!" cried
Uncle Wiggily. "What does that mean? You
startle and puzzle me."

"Why, you know the circus elephant has to
dress up like a clown," went on Peetie. "And
he plays a drum and a handorgan, and he fires
off a cannon in the sawdust ring. And he does
a lot of things like that. After a while his white
clown suit gets all dirt and he has to wash out his
clothes. Then he has to squeeze them in a
wringer to get as much of the water out as he can.
Then he hangs them up to dry.

"Well, he can turn the wringer himself with
his trunk, but his paws are so big that he can't
put the clothes through between the rubber
rollers. So he advertised for some little animal
boy to help him after school. I answered, and
I'm going to help him wash and dry his clothes."

"How much are you to get?" asked Uncle
Wiggily.

"I get three puppy biscuits every day and a
glass of pink lemonade, and on Saturday after-
noons I can go to the circus for nothing."

"Fine!" cried Uncle Wiggily. "I'm real
glad you came to tell me. You are good and
smart little animal boys."

Then Peetie and Jackie ran off to do the new

work they had arranged for, and Uncle Wiggily cleaned his auto ready for his ride next day. And when he had finished he thought he would take a walk down to the circus tent and see how Peetie was helping the elephant wash the clothes. As for Jackie, he had to run so fast, here and there and everywhere, to deliver his papers that Uncle Wiggily did not know where to find him, any more than Bo-peep did her sheep.

Well, in a little while, the rabbit gentleman came to where the elephant was washing his clothes. Of course he had to have a very large tub and washboard and an extra large wringer for his clothes were very large.

And there, up on a box in front of the tub, that was filled with suds and water, stood Peetie Bow Wow, splashing around, and reaching down in for the wet clothes. And as he fished them up, and put the ends between the rubber rollers of the wringer, the elephant would turn the handle of the squee-gee machine with his trunk.

" How is that? " asked Peetie.

" Fine! " cried the elephant, making his trunk go faster and faster, and squirting the water out of the wet clothes, all over the ground.

" Yes, Peetie is a good little chap," said Uncle Wiggily. Just then the elephant's brother came along, and the two big animals began talking together. And, as they were both a little deaf, each one shouted to the other as loudly as he could. Oh! such a racket as they made—thunder was nothing to it!

And then a funny thing happened. Peetie turned around to put some more clothes in the tub, when, all of a sudden, his tail got caught in between the wringer's rubber rollers.

"Ouch!" cried the little puppy dog. "Ouch! Oh, dear me! Stop, please, Mr. Elephant. Don't turn the wringer any more!"

But the two elephants were talking together, each one as loudly as he could, about how much hay they could eat, and how some little boys at a circus would give them only one peanut instead of a whole bag full, and all things like that. So the clothes-washing elephant never noticed that Peetie's tail was caught in the rollers. And he didn't hear him cry.

Around and around the elephant turned the handle of the wringer with his trunk, winding Peetie's tail right between the rollers, and drawing the little puppy dog boy himself closer and closer into the tub, over the water and nearer to the rubber rollers themselves.

"Oh, stop! Oh, stop!" cried poor Peetie trying to get away, but he could not. "If I get rolled between the rollers I'll be as flat as a pancake!" he screamed. "Oh, stop! Oh, Uncle Wiggily, save me!"

"Yes, I will!" cried the rabbit gentleman. "You must stop turning that wringer!" he said to the circus elephant. "You are wringing Peetie instead of the clothes. His tail is caught!"

But the elephant was so deaf, and his brother was calling to him so loudly about pink lemonade, that he could not hear either Peetie or Uncle Wiggily. Then, to make him listen, Uncle Wiggily with his crutch tickled the elephant's foot, which was as high up as he could reach, but the big creature thought it was only a mosquito, and paid no attention.

"Oh, what shall I do?" cried Peetie.

"I'll save you!" exclaimed Uncle Wiggily, and then, happening to have a bag of peanuts in his pocket he held them close to the elephant's trunk. The elephant could smell, if he could not hear well, and all at once he took the peanuts, and as he did so, of course, he removed his trunk from the wringer handle.

And as he ate the peanuts he saw what a terrible thing he was doing, wringing Peetie instead of the clothes, so he very kindly made the wringer go backwards, and out came Peetie's tail again, a little flat, but not much hurt otherwise.

"I am so sorry," said the elephant. "I wouldn't have had it happen for the world."

"Yes, it was an accident," spoke Uncle Wiggily, "but I guess Peetie had better find some other kind of work to do after school."

"All right," said the elephant. "I'll pay him off, and then I'll get a rubbery snake to help me with my clothes. A snake won't mind being squeezed."

So he did that, and Peetie and Uncle Wiggily went home, and nothing more happened that day. But next, in case the automobile horn doesn't blow the little girl's rubber balloon up in the top of the tree, where the kittie cat has its nest, I'll tell you about Uncle Wiggily and the trained nurse.

STORY XVII

UNCLE WIGGILY AND THE TRAINED NURSE

UNCLE WIGGILY LONGEARS, the gentleman
rabbit, was out riding in his automobile. He was
taking exercise, so he would not be so fat, for a
fat rabbit is about the fattest thing there is, except a balloon, and that doesn't count, as it has
no ears.

" I wonder what will happen to me to-day?"
said Uncle Wiggily, as he rode along, turning
the turnip steering wheel from one side to the
other to keep from bumping into stones and
stumps, and things like that. And, every now
and then, Uncle Wiggily would take a bite out
of his turnip steering wheel. That was what it
was for, you see. And as for the German bologna
sausages which were the tires. Uncle Wiggily
used to let anybody who wanted to—such as a
hungry doggie or a starving kittie—take a bite
out of them whenever they wanted to.

Well, pretty soon, after a while, not so very

long, Uncle Wiggily came to the top of a hill.
He stopped his auto there to look around at the
green fields and the apple trees in blossom, and at
the little brook running along over the green,
mossy stones. And the brook never stubbed its
toe once on the stones! What do you think of
that?

" Well, I guess I'll go down hill," thought the
old gentleman rabbit, and down he started.

But Oh unhappiness! Sadness, and, also, isn't
it too bad!

No sooner had Uncle Wiggily started down
the hill in his auto than the snicker-snooker-um
got twisted around the boodle-oodle-um, and that
made the wibble-wobble-ton stand on its head,
instead of standing on its ear as it really ought to
have done.

Then the auto ran away, and the next thing
Uncle Wiggily knew his car had hit a stump,
turned a somersault and part of a peppersault,
and he was thrown out.

" Bang! " he fell, right on the hard ground, and
for a moment he stayed there, being too much out
of breath to get up and see what was the matter.

And when he tried to get up he couldn't.
Something had happened to him. He had hit his
head on a stone. Poor Uncle Wiggily!

But, very luckily. Dr. Possum happened to

be passing, having just come from paying a
visit to Grandfather Goosey Gander, who had,
by mistake, eaten a shoe button with his corn
meal pudding. And Dr. Possum, having cured
Grandpa Goosey, went at once to help Uncle
Wiggily.

"We must get you home right away, Uncle
Wiggily," said the doctor gentleman. "You
must be put to bed and have a trained nurse."

"Well, as long as I have to have a nurse, I
should much prefer," said Uncle Wiggily,
faintly, "I should much prefer a trained one to a
wild one. For a trained nurse who can do tricks
will be quite funny."

"Hum!" exclaimed Dr. Possum. "A trained
nurse has no time to do tricks. Now rest yourself."

So Uncle Wiggily sat back quietly in Dr.
Possum's auto until he got to his hollow stump
home. Then Old Dog Percival and the doctor
carried the rabbit gentleman in, and they sent for
a trained nurse. For Uncle Wiggily was quite
badly hurt, and needed some one to feed him for
a while.

Pretty soon the trained nurse came, and who
did she turn out to be but Nurse Jane Fuzzy
Wuzzy herself, the kind old muskrat. She had
been living with Uncle Wiggily, but, for a time,

had gone off to study to be a trained nurse. She put on a white cap and a blue and white striped dress, and she was just as good a nurse as one could get from the hospital. Uncle Wiggily was too ill to notice, though.

"I know how to look after him," said Nurse Jane, and she really did.

She felt of his pulse, and made him put out his tongue to look at, to see that he had not swallowed it by mistake, and she found out how hot he was to see if he had fever, and all things like that. And she put a report of all these things down on a bit of white birch bark for paper, using a licorice stick for a pencil. Afterward Dr. Possum would read the report.

Well, for some time Uncle Wiggily was quite ill, for you know it is no fun to be in an automobile accident. Then he began to get better. Nurse Jane did not have much to do, and Dr. Possum, who came in every day, said:

"He will get well now. But Uncle Wiggily has had a hard time of it; very hard!"

And, as soon as he began to get better, Uncle Wiggily got sort of impatient, and he wanted many things he could not have, or which were not good for him. He wanted to get out of bed, but Nurse Jane would not let him, for the doctor had told her not to.

Then Uncle Wiggily said:

"Well, you are a trained nurse. Now you must do some tricks for me, or I shall get out of bed whether you want me to or not," and he barked like a dog; really he did. You see he was not exactly himself, but rather out of his head on account of the fever. "Come on, do some tricks!" he cried to Nurse Jane.

Poor Miss Fuzzy-Wuzzy! She had never done a trick since she was a little girl muskrat, but she knew sick rabbits must be humored, so she tried to think of a trick. She did not know whether to make believe jump rope, play puss in a corner or pretend that she was a fire engine. And she really wanted to help Uncle Wiggily!

"Come on! Do something!" he cried, and he almost jumped out of bed. "Do something."

And just then, as it happened, a great big bee flew in the window, and maybe it was going to sting Uncle Wiggily, for all I know. Then Nurse Jane knew what to do.

She caught up a soft towel, so as not to hurt the bee any more than she had to, and she began hitting at him.

"Get out of here! Get out of here!" cried Nurse Jane. "You can't sting Uncle Wiggily!"

"Buzz! Buzz!" sang the bee.

"Go out! Go out!" exclaimed Nurse Jane, and she made the towel sail through the air. The bee flew this way and that, up and down and sideways, but always Nurse Jane was after him with the towel, trying to drive him out of the window.

She climbed up on chairs, she jumped over tables, without knocking over a single medicine bottle. She crawled under the sofa and out again, she even jumped on the couch and bounced up in the air like a balloon. And at last she drove the bad bee out doors where he could get honey from the flowers, and they didn't mind his stinging them if he wanted to, which of course he didn't.

Then, after that, Nurse Jane Fuzzy Wuzzy sat down in a chair, near Uncle Wiggily, very tired out indeed. The old gentleman rabbit opened his eyes and laughed a little.

"Those were funny tricks you did for me," he said, "jumping around like that. Very funny! Ha! Ha!"

"I was not doing tricks," answered Nurse Jane, surprised-like. "I was trying to keep a bee from biting you."

"Were you indeed?" spoke Uncle Wiggily. "I thought they were some of the tricks you had been trained to do. They were fine. I laughed so hard that I think I am much better."

And, indeed, he was, and soon he was all well, so that Nurse Jane Fuzzy, without really meaning to at all, had done some funny tricks when she drove out that bee. Oh! trained nurses are very queer, I think, but they are very nice, also.

So Uncle Wiggily was soon well, and needed no nurse, and when his auto was mended, he could ride around in it as nicely as before.

STORY XVIII

UNCLE WIGGILY AND THE DENTIST

ONE morning Uncle Wiggily, the old gentleman rabbit, awoke so suddenly that he nearly fell out of bed. He gave a jump, and put one of his paws to his mouth, exclaiming:

"My! Oh, my! What can be the matter? Such a pain! Oh, double wow!" and whenever Uncle Wiggily said double wow, instead of single, you might know something extra-extraordinary had happened, such as that the roof had blown off, or that the cat was having a fit. But it was neither of those things this time. It was a dreadful pain that Uncle Wiggily had.

"Why, what can be the matter with me?" the rabbit gentleman went on. "Oh, what an ache! Nurse Jane!" he called, as he slipped into his dressing gown and fairly tumbled into his slippers. "Come here, Nurse Jane Fuzzy-Wuzzy!" he begged. The kind muskrat lady was staying with the rabbit gentleman for a while once more.

"Why, whatever can have happened?" asked

the muskrat. " Has the bed fallen down, or has
a mosquito bitten you? "

" Worse and worse! " cried Uncle Wiggily.
" I have such a pain in my tooth. I must have
caught cold when I was out riding in my automobile yesterday. Oh, double wow! "

Nurse Jane Fuzzy-Wuzzy came hurrying up-
stairs from the kitchen, where she was baking
some carrot pancakes for breakfast. She was not
a trained nurse any longer, and she did not wear
the white cap and the blue and white striped
dress. She was just a plain nurse, not a trained
one, now.

" Oh, please do something for me! " begged
Uncle Wiggily, jumping up and down from the
pain so that the tassels on his bathrobe went
flippity-flop, like a little girl's braids of hair when
she jumps the skipping rope.

" Open your mouth," said Nurse Jane.

Uncle Wiggily did so.

" Why, you have a hole in one of your teeth,"
went on Miss Fuzzy-Wuzzy. " You will have to
go to the dentist's and have it filled."

" Filled with what? " asked Uncle Wiggily, as
he jumped harder than ever. " Ice cream? "

" Mercy me, no! " answered Nurse Jane.
" That would make it ache worse than ever. You
see the tooth has a hole in it, and the cold air, and

the cold water you drink, touch on the nerve, and
that makes it ache."

"So I have a toothache; is that it?" asked
Uncle Wiggily.

"You have—and a bad one," replied Nurse
Jane.

"And I shall have to go to the dentist's?"

"You will. But don't worry. He will stop
up the hole and you will be all better."

"Oh, dear! I do seem to have the most lot of
trouble!" cried Uncle Wiggily. "Well, if I
have to go I have to. I'll start right out and see
what happens. But I wonder what he will use
to fill up that hole?"

"Oh, cotton, or rubber, or gold or silver!"
answered Nurse Jane.

"I think I will take gold," said Uncle Wiggily. "Then, no matter how poor I get, I will
always have some gold in my tooth. Yes, I'll
choose gold."

So off he went to the dentist's office. The
dentist was a nice bear gentleman, kind and good,
who had long claws so that he could pull out an
aching tooth if he had to. But mostly he filled
teeth instead of pulling them out, for it is too
bad to have to pull a tooth if you can save it.

"Get into this chair, and we will see what is the
trouble," spoke the bear dentist. So Uncle Wig-

gily sat in the chair, and pretty soon he went up—up just as in an elevator.

" Why—why—what happened? " he asked in surprise, and his tooth didn't ache so much now.

" Oh, I just raised the chair up a bit so I could look into your mouth more easily," replied the kind dentist. " You see, my chair I can make high or low as I wish, by pushing on a what-you-may-call-it. I make it high for little animals and low for big ones, like elephants and the like of that."

" Do elephants ever have toothache? " asked Uncle Wiggily, curious-like.

" Indeed they do! " exclaimed the bear dentist. " Why, I had one in here once and I had to use a bushel of shavings to fill a hole in his large tooth, so he could eat peanuts without getting a spasm."

" My! My! " exclaimed Uncle Wiggily, and his pain was not quite so bad now, for you see he was thinking of something else.

" Well, I'll not have to put much gold in that hole in your tooth," went on the dentist bear. " It is a small one."

" It feels large," said Uncle Wiggily, putting the point of his tongue in it. " It feels as big as a shoe."

" It always does," replied the dentist. So he

got ready to fill Uncle Wiggily's tooth. First he used a thing like a buzz saw, only different. That was to brush out the hole, and make it nice and clean, just like when mamma dusts the parlor chairs because company is coming. Then the dentist put some cotton, with some nice smelling stuff on it, in the tooth.

"Does it hurt much?" he asked Uncle Wiggily.

"Yes, quite a bit. But—I—I—can stand it," and with his paws Uncle Wiggily took tight hold of the arms of the chair.

"It will soon be over," said the bear dentist. All dentists say that—even papa's and mamma's kind.

Then he put some gold in Uncle Wiggily's hollow tooth and pushed it in hard, so that it would not come out. Then he did a lot of other funny things, and squirted some perfumery in the mouth of the rabbit gentleman, and a nice lady bear dentist who was in the next room, came in and helped hold Uncle Wiggily's mouth open, for he was tired of holding it himself.

"There you are—all done!" suddenly exclaimed the good bear dentist. "Now it won't ache you again!"

"I am so glad of that," spoke Uncle Wiggily.

Well, he was just paying the dentist bear gentleman some money, when, all of a sudden, the door of the office opened, and in came a great big skillery-scalery alligator on the jump.

" Oh! " cried the alligator. " Such a toothache! Such a toothache! Oh, I must bite on somebody! I guess I'll bite on you! " and he looked at Uncle Wiggily. " No, I guess I'll bite on you," and he looked at the bear gentleman dentist. " No, I'll bite on you! " he cried to the lady bear dentist, and really you could not blame him, for she was very nice.

Then the alligator jumped up and down, and waggled his tail so hard that he knocked over a vase of flowers, and cried out:

" Oh, what a toothache! I guess I'll bite all three of you! I must bite some one. I'll bite all of you! "

" Oh, my! " exclaimed Uncle Wiggily. " This is terrible! What shall I do? "

The alligator made a jump for the rabbit gentleman, but the bear dentist caught the skillery-scalery creature by his flipping-flapping tail, and said:

" Here! You let Uncle Wiggily alone! I know what is the matter with you. That toothache has made you so upset and kerslastrated that you don't know what you are doing. That's all— you are not yourself. But I will fix you! "

"Fix me! What will you do?" cried the alligator, holding a clawy paw to his long jaw.

"I will stop your toothache and then you will be a good alligator instead of a bad one, and not want to bite any one," said the bear dentist, and he did so, and when the alligator's tooth stopped aching, which it soon did, he was as good as pie, and so gentle that he even did not want to bite the end off his ice cream cone.

So that's how Uncle Wiggily went to the dentist's, and I've told you all that happened there, even about the skillery-scalery alligator. And on the page after this, in case the moving picture man doesn't take our kitchen sink away to use for a fountain pen, I'll tell you about Uncle Wiggily and the baby rabbit.

STORY XIX

UNCLE WIGGILY AND THE BABY RABBIT

"Well, how are you to-day?" asked Dr. Possum of Uncle Wiggily, the old gentleman rabbit, as the physician stopped in front of the rabbit gentleman's hollow stump house. "Are you coming on pretty well?"

"Pretty well, yes, I thank you," said Uncle Wiggily. "I have gotten all over being ill, and my toothache has stopped, thanks to the bear dentist. I don't know what may happen next."

"I can tell you," said Dr. Possum, looking in his bag to see if he had any bitter-sweet medicine for Lulu Wibblewobble, the duck girl, who had a gumboil on her foot.

"What?" asked Uncle Wiggily.

"You will get so fat that you can't even see your shoes—to say nothing of lacing them," spoke the doctor. "You are not taking exercise enough. You must ride around in your auto more."

"But," answered Uncle Wiggily, "ever since

the time when I got the toothache, I have been a little afraid of going out much, you see."

"Nonsensicalness! I don't see anything of the kind," spoke Dr. Possum. "You must go out for a ride."

"All right—if, you say so," sighed Uncle Wiggily. "I will go to-morrow."

"You must go to-day!" insisted the doctor animal. "There is no use putting off anything that has to be done. Go right away!"

"I will!" promised Uncle Wiggily.

So, in a little while, the old gentleman rabbit was off in his auto, making the tinkerum-tankerum go like anything, and the whizzicum-whazzicum fairly turn peppersaults. And Dr. Possum went to see how Lulu Wibblewobble's gumboil on her foot was getting along. I think it was a gumboil, but I'm not sure.

Anyhow, Uncle Wiggily rode on and on, over the fields and through the woods, until, all of a sudden, he heard a little crying noise, such as when you step on a rubber ball in the dark, and it squeaks.

"My! What can that be!" exclaimed Uncle Wiggily.

Once more the crying noise sounded. It seemed to come from a hollow stump, near a big rock.

"Ha! Can that stump have the toothache, as I had?" asked the old gentleman rabbit. "No, that cannot be—stumps have no teeth. I must look into this."

So he stopped his auto and went over toward the hollow stump, and the crying noise kept up, being quite pitiful this time.

"Oh, dear!" said Uncle Wiggily. "It sounds like a baby. Whatever in the world will I do with a baby?"

But still he was a brave old gentleman rabbit, and he went closer to the hollow stump. Looking down in it he saw, all nestled up in some soft brown leaves, a tiny baby rabbit.

"Wah! Wah! Wah!" cried the baby.

"You poor little creature!" exclaimed Uncle Wiggily. "No one to look after you! I guess I'll have to do it myself."

So he picked up the baby rabbit, wrapped it up in his big red handkerchief, Uncle Wiggily did, for the baby rabbit had on only a little, thin white dress, and it was quite cool that day.

"Where do you live, little baby?" asked Uncle Wiggily. "I think you are lost, and I'll take you home."

"Wah! Wah!" cried the baby.

"Ha! That is a new language to me!" said Uncle Wiggily. "I cannot speak it. I do not understand it. Still, I will take you along in my auto, and maybe we will meet your papa or mamma looking for you."

"Wah! Wah!" cried the baby.

"You keep saying the same thing over and over again," said Uncle Wiggily. "Never mind, I suppose you cannot help it."

So he got in his auto with the baby rabbit and started off, holding the little creature on his lap, well wrapped up in a robe. The baby rabbit had stopped crying now, and it was playing with the dingleum-dangleum on the steering wheel turnip. Then it tried to bite a piece out of the turnip itself.

"No, no!" exclaimed Uncle Wiggily. "Baby mustn't do that! Baby naughty!"

"Wah! Wah!" cried the baby, doubling up like a peanut.

"There you go again," exclaimed Uncle Wiggily. "I'm sure I don't know what to do with you."

"Wah!" said the baby.

Uncle Wiggily made his auto go faster, and pretty soon he came to the place where Sammie and Susie Littletail, the rabbit children, lived.

"I'll stop there," he thought, "and see if they know where this baby belongs, and what I can do to make him stop crying."

So Uncle Wiggily did this, and as soon as Susie Littletail saw that cute little baby rabbit, she exclaimed:

"Oh, mamma! Mayn't we keep it? I'd love to have a baby brother or sister. Can't I keep it?" And she cuddled the lost baby rabbit in her arms.

"Keep it? No, certainly not. The idea!" cried Mrs. Littletail. "No, Susie!"

"Wah! Wah! Wah!" cried the baby.

"That's the way it's been going ever since I found it in the hollow stump," said Uncle Wiggily, sadly-like. "It is quite distressing; what shall I do?"

"I'll take care of it," said Mrs. Littletail. "I think it must be hungry. "I'll give it some carrots and milk."

So she began to warm the milk, and Uncle Wiggily sat and watched Susie hold the baby. He was glad some one knew how to take care of it, and he hoped the little rabbit's mamma and papa would soon come for it.

All of a sudden the door opened and a sneaking old fox poked his head in. He looked at Uncle Wiggily and then at Mrs. Littletail, and then at Susie and then at the baby, which was not crying now.

"I wonder which one I shall grab first?"

thought the fox. " I must have one of them. I think I will take the baby."

And neither Susie, nor Uncle Wiggily, nor Mrs. Littletail, nor the baby saw the sneaking fox. The baby's eyes were shut and all the others had their backs turned. The fox crept up behind Susie, and he was just going to grab the baby, when the little thing suddenly awakened and cried out.

" Wah! Wah! Goo! Moo! Bur-r-r-r! Oh, wah! Wah-wah! Ooo-oo! Scoo! Blink! Blank! Blunk!" cried the baby rabbit.

" Oh, my!" exclaimed the sneaky-eaky fox. " As bad as that, eh? I don't want that kind of a baby. It would keep me awake all night," and away the fox ran so fast that he nearly lost his tail, and so he didn't get any one to eat, after all.

Then Mrs. Littletail fixed the milk and carrots for the baby rabbit, and it went to sleep and didn't cry any more. And soon its mamma came looking for it. She had left it in the hollow stump while she did her washing, only Uncle Wiggily came along and mixed matters up, though he did not mean to, by taking the baby away.

But everything came out right, and in the story after this one, in case the boy selling pea-

nuts at the front door doesn't forget to bring me
a few, striped red, white and blue, like a circus
elephant. I'll tell you about Uncle Wiggily and
his spectacles.

STORY XX

UNCLE WIGGILY'S SPECTACLES

UNCLE WIGGILY, the nice old gentleman rabbit, was asleep in a big easy chair in the sitting-
room of the Wibblewobble duck house where he
had gone for a little visit. It was daytime, but
Uncle Wiggily was taking a nap. He was
dreaming of riding out in his new automobile and
he was sleeping very nicely, when, all at once,
along came Jimmie Wibblewobble, the boy duck,
and Sammie Littletail, the boy rabbit, was with
him. They had just come home from school.

They looked in the sitting-room and saw
Uncle Wiggily asleep in front of the fire. There
was no one else in the house just then, as Mrs.
Wibblewobble had gone down to the five and ten
cent store to buy a new piano.

"Oh, look at Uncle Wiggily!" exclaimed
Sammie. "He hasn't gotten very far on his
travels if he's only at your house."

"We like him to stay here very much," said

Jimmie. " Please don't talk aloud and wake
him up."

" Oh, look! " exclaimed Sammie, " Uncle Wiggily's glasses have fallen off his twinkling nose
and are on the carpet."

" So they are," said Jimmie. " I'll go in and
pick up his spectacles so he won't step on them
and break them when he wakes."

" Wait! Hold on! " exclaimed Sammie, with
a whispering laugh. " I know how we can have
some fun."

" How? " asked Jimmie, who always liked to
have a good time.

" Why, we'll go in there very softly and get
Uncle Wiggily's glasses. Then we'll get a
picture book, or paper, and we'll cut out a little
picture of a bear and another picture of a wolf,
and we'll paste the pictures on Uncle Wiggily's
glasses. Then when he wakes up and puts them
on he'll think he sees a bear and a wolf, and he'll
holler like anything, and maybe make believe
shoot them, for he is very brave, you know; and
we'll hide behind the door and listen, and it will
be a jolly joke."

" Won't it hurt him? " asked Jimmie, thought-
like.

" Not a bit! " exclaimed Sammie. " I wouldn't

hurt Uncle Wiggily for a million dollars. And
it won't even scare him, as he is so brave."

"Then we'll do it," agreed Jimmie, "and I
hope he won't be angry at us for playing the
trick."

"Oh, he won't," spoke Sammie. So into the
sitting-room they went, very softly, and they
took up the spectacles from the carpet. Then
they went up to the playroom and got an old
picture book, and out of it they cut a bear and a
wolf, not real, you know, but make believe.

Then Jimmie pasted the picture of a wolf on
one of the glasses of Uncle Wiggily's spectacles,
and Sammie pasted the picture of a bear on the
other glass. And, just as they were almost
finished, what do you think happened? Why,
Lulu and Alice Wibblewobble, the two duck
girls, came in, very, very softly, and they saw
what those two boys were doing.

"Oh, what do you think of that?" asked Alice
of Lulu, in a whisper.

"They're playing a joke on Uncle Wiggily,"
said Lulu, as she peeked into the room where
Sammie and Jimmie were. "I wish we could
play a joke on those boys."

"Perhaps we can," suggested Alice. "We'll
just keep very quiet and watch."

So they watched, and they saw Jimmie and Sammie go back down to the sitting-room and put the glasses on the carpet just where they had first fallen. And Uncle Wiggily was still asleep with his eyes shut.

" Now we'll go hide," said Sammie to Jimmie, " and when Uncle Wiggily wakes up and puts on his glasses he'll think he sees a wolf and a bear. Come and hide, Jimmie, and we'll see some fun."

" First, let's go down to the kitchen and get some cookies," said Jimmie, the boy duck. " Mamma always leaves some for me when I come from school."

" Cookies! Oh, goodie! Yum-yum!" exclaimed Sammie, so the boy duck and the boy rabbit went down to the Wibblewobble kitchen.

" Now is our chance!" exclaimed Alice to Lulu, for, you see, they had been watching the boys through a crack in the door all this while.

" What are you going to do?" asked Lulu.

" I'm going to get Uncle Wiggily's glasses, take off the picture of the bear and wolf, and in place of them you and I will paste a picture of some lovely flowers on one glass and on the other we'll put a picture of a chocolate cake with a carrot on top."

" Oh, that will be fun, and we'll fool Jimmie

and Sammie!" said Lulu. So those two girl ducks went in the room very softly, got the glasses from the floor, and took them out. Then they cut from one picture book a bunch of flowers and from another book a chocolate-cake picture. These they pasted on the glasses, and then they put the spectacles back where Uncle Wiggily would find them when he woke up.

"Now we'll hide and watch," said Alice to Lulu. So they hid behind one door, and pretty soon Jimmie and Sammie came back from the kitchen, and the boys hid behind another door. Then pretty soon Uncle Wiggily awakened and he waved his ears backward and frontward, and he twinkled his nose like a star on a frosty night, and then he got up.

"My goodness!" he suddenly exclaimed. "My glasses! Where are they?" Then he looked down and saw them on the floor. "Ha! It's a good thing I didn't step on them," he said.

Then he put the glasses on, and Jimmie nudged Sammie in the ribsie-ibsie and exclaimed in a whisper:

"Now watch him!"

And then Uncle Wiggily gave a jump and cried out:

"Oh, how lovely! What a delicious chocolate cake I see! And what a fine carrot on top.

And what beautiful flowers! Oh, I wonder if they are real? And if that chocolate cake is real. Oh! Oh! Won't I just eat it, though!" Then he saw that it was only some pictures pasted on his glasses, and the rabbit gentleman laughed and cried out:

"Ha! Ha! That is a joke of some of the children, I know. But it was a very nice joke. I wonder who put the flowers and cake pictures on my glasses?"

"We did, if you please," said Alice and Lulu, stepping out from behind the door just then.

"Oh, you are very kind," said Uncle Wiggily, "and here is five cents for each of you." Then he gave them the money.

"Well, what do you think about that?" asked Sammie of Jimmie, real surprised-like.

"Something went wrong," said the boy duck.

"I should say so," said Sammie. "Say," he asked, as he stepped out from behind the door, "isn't there a picture of a wolf and a bear on your glasses, Uncle Wiggily?"

"A wolf and a bear? Oh, you little rascally boys!" cried the old gentleman rabbit. "I see how it happened. Alice and Lulu got ahead of you and spoiled your joke, didn't they?"

"Yes," said Jimmie and Sammie, "they did.

But we didn't mean to scare you, Uncle
Wiggily."

" Oh, I know you didn't," he said, " so here is
five cents for each of you boys." Then all the
animal children went downtown and bought
chocolate sodas, and Uncle Wiggily washed his
glasses clean, and that's the end of this story,
if you please.

But on the page after this, in case the little
boy downstairs doesn't pound a hole in the ceil-
ing with his fish pole and break my typewriter
ribbon, so the rag doll can't wear it to the picnic,
I'll tell you about Uncle Wiggily and the big
carrot.

STORY XXI

UNCLE WIGGILY AND THE CARROT

"DON'T you want to come for a ride through the woods in my automobile?" asked Uncle Wiggily Longears, one morning, of Alice and Lulu and Jimmie Wibblewobble, the duck children.

"Oh, that will be lovely!" exclaimed Alice. "I wonder what color hair ribbon I shall wear?"

"Put on any color," said Jimmie, "and don't fuss so. We want to get started some time today."

"Oh, very well," answered his sister. So she put on a blue banana-colored hair ribbon and soon she was ready to go off with Uncle Wiggily.

"Oh, but wait a minute!" suddenly exclaimed Mrs. Wibblewobble. "I almost forgot. I won't be here when you come back for dinner, as I am going downtown with Mrs. Goat, Billie's and Nannie's mother, you know. Now, I'll fix the lunch all ready for you and leave it on the din-

ing-room table, and you can get it yourselves
when you return from your auto ride. There is
some cherry pie for Uncle Wiggily, and
some——"

"Don't say another word!" cried the old
gentleman rabbit, in delight. "I know what
we will do. We'll take our lunch with us in the
auto and eat it in the woods. It's a little cool,
but we can build a fire and we'll be warm."

"Oh, fine and dandy!" cried Jimmie. "That's
just great!"

"I think so, too," spoke Lulu, but Alice was
so busy tying her hair ribbon into a big bow
just then, and besides she had a hairpin in her
beak, so she couldn't say anything. But she
liked the idea, I guess. Soon they were ready
to start off with their lunch in a basket, and
there was some specially fine cherry pie for Uncle
Wiggily.

Well, they traveled on and on in the auto, and
Mrs. Wibblewobble had gone downtown shopping with Mrs. Goat, and everything was as
lovely as it could be. Pretty soon Uncle Wiggily and the children came to a nice place in the
woods where the brown leaves covered the
ground, and where there were a lot of trees so
close together that the wind didn't blow through
'em too strong, and make it cold.

" Ah, here is a good place to build our fire and
have lunch," said the old gentleman rabbit.
" Jimmie, you gather some wood for the blaze.
Lulu, you find a nice flat stump that will do for
the table. Alice, you spread the tablecloth, and
set the stump-table, and then you and Lulu can
get the things to eat out of the basket."

" And what are you going to do, Uncle Wiggily? " asked Jimmie, the boy duck.

" Oh, I am going to walk around and see if I
can find a spring of water where we can get some
to drink, and I also want to put some in my auto,
for it is thirsty and needs cooling off. And I
may find some water-cress for us to eat, too,"
went on the old gentleman rabbit.

So he walked off through the woods, and
Jimmie began to gather sticks of wood in his
strong yellow bill, and Lulu and Alice found a
nice stump and set it for the table.

And then, all at once, as Jimmie was walking
along, he saw something long and yellow lying
on the ground, and he cried out:

" Oh, Uncle Wiggily! Come here quick!
Wow! Wow! Hurry up! "

" What is it, a snake? " asked the old gentleman rabbit.

" No, it isn't a snake," answered Jimmie.
" It's a big, yellow carrot, the largest I have ever

seen.   It will be just fine for our dinner, cut up in chunks."

So Uncle Wiggily, who had just found a nice, cool spring of water, ran over to where Jimmie was, and surely enough there on the ground was a big yellow carrot.

"My!" exclaimed the old gentleman rabbit. "That surely is the largest one I have ever come across.   It must have grown on a giant's farm," for the carrot was about as long as a clothes post and as big around as a barrel of apples.

"Can we take it for our lunch?" asked Jimmie.

"I guess so; yes," said Uncle Wiggily.   "But we can never lift it.   Ha!   I have it.   I will tie a string to it and fasten the string to my auto and then I'll pull the giant carrot along to where we are going to eat, and we can easily cut it up for dinner.   And what we have left we'll take home."

So he brought up his auto and steered it to where the big carrot lay on the ground.   Then he fastened the yellow vegetable to the machine by a strong cord and started to drag the carrot along.   And then all of a sudden the string broke.

"Wait!   Wait!" cried Jimmie, who was watching.   "I must tie the string."   And then

a very funny thing happened. All of a sudden
that carrot just stood straight up on end and it
began hopping around, and then it did a little
dance and jig, and then it stretched out on the
ground again, and rolled over and over like a
horse in the meadow, scratching his back.

" Oh, wow! " cried Jimmie. " Look at that! "

" Whatever is the matter with the carrot? "
asked Alice.

" It's a fairy carrot, that's what it is," said
Lulu.

" Ha! It certainly is very strange," said
Uncle Wiggily.

And then from inside the carrot came a jolly
shout.

" Ha! Ha! " laughed some one, and then the
carrot all at once seemed to come apart, and out
from inside of it stepped Billie and Johnnie
Bushytail, the boy squirrels.

" Oh, what a fine joke," cried Billie.

" What! Isn't that a real carrot? " asked
Uncle Wiggily.

" No, it's only one made of cloth, stuffed with
dried leaves, and then we got inside so as to make
it wiggle," said Johnnie.

" Why, what in the world did you do that
for? " asked Lulu.

" Oh, we started to make a balloon of yellow

cloth," said the squirrel boys, " but it wasn't any good, and it wouldn't go up. So we thought we'd make believe it was a giant carrot, and we got in it, though we never thought you'd come along and find us. But I'm glad you did."

" Yes," added Jonnie, " for I smell cherry pie."

" So you do! " said Uncle Wiggily, " and you shall have some. My, that was a good joke, all right! No wonder I couldn't pull the big carrot with you squirrel boys inside."

So they all went back to the stump-table, and they built a fire and had a fine lunch there in the woods, and it was very good, even if they didn't have any carrot. Then Billie and Johnnie took the leaf stuffing out of the yellow cloth that they had made, hoping it would be a balloon and go up to the sky, and they all got in Uncle Wiggily's auto and went home.

Now in case it doesn't snow pop-corn balls, and scare my pussy cat, so that she jumps up on top of the clothes-post, I'll tell you next about Uncle Wiggily and the pancakes.

STORY XXII

UNCLE WIGGILY AND THE PANCAKES

ONE fine frosty morning Uncle Wiggily went out to the barn to turn the whizzicum-whazzicum on his auto right side up, for in the night a rat had slept on it and bent it over backward.

" I think I will ride over and see Grandfather Goosey Gander this morning," said the old gentleman rabbit, when he had put some gasoline in the tinkerum-tankerum.

" And may we go with you? " asked Jimmie Wibblewobble, the polite little duck boy, who came out to get some cornmeal, for his mamma was going to make buckwheat cakes for breakfast that morning, and sometimes she put in them a little cornmeal, I don't know why or I'd tell you. Anyhow she did it.

" Oh, I'm afraid you can't come this morning," said Uncle Wiggily, kindly. " You know it isn't Saturday, and you and Alice and Lulu must go to school. Some other time you may come."

Well, Jimmie thought it would be rather more

fun to go off auto riding, than to go to school, but still he got his books together and did a little studying before breakfast.

And what a fine breakfast it was, with lots of buckwheat cakes and maple syrup and sausage gravy and coffee made of barley and roasted corn. Well, I'm afraid to tell you how many pancakes Lulu and Alice and Jimmie and Mr. Wibblewobble ate. And Uncle Wiggily himself ate quite a number, too. Of course, no one was greedy, but the pancakes, or griddle cakes, as some folks call them, were very, very good.

"There I haven't any more to bake!" finally exclaimed Mrs. Wibblewobble, with a laugh. "You'll all have to stop eating."

So they did, and soon the children went off to school, and Mr. Wibblewobble went to work in the feather factory, and Uncle Wiggily went off in his auto to call on Grandfather Goosey Gander, for he hadn't seen the old gentleman duck in a long, long time.

Well, pretty soon, in a little while, not so very long, Uncle Wiggily came to the place where Grandfather Goosey Gander lived. He knocked on the door and, instead of some one coming to open it, a voice called out:

"Walk in! Walk in!"

"My goodness me sakes alive!" thought Uncle Wiggily. "Who is that?"

Then the voice called again:

"Come in! Come in! Why don't you come in? I'm hungry, so very hungry!"

"Oh, dear!" exclaimed Uncle Wiggily. "That doesn't sound like Grandfather Goosey Gander's voice. Perhaps a bad fox has gotten in and is hiding there now, waiting for some one else to come in, so he can eat them up. I'd better run and tell the policeman dog."

Well, Uncle Wiggily was just going to run back to his auto, when he happened to look in through the window, and there he saw Grandfather Goosey sitting on a chair by the stove, and the old gentleman duck had his feet in a basin of hot water.

"Ha! Grandfather Goosey is ill!" exclaimed the rabbit gentleman. "I'll go in." So in he went, and he asked: "What is the matter, Grandfather? Can I help you?"

"Oh, I have a dreadful cold," said Grandfather Goosey, "and I am as hoarse as a crow."

"That's why it didn't sound like your voice," said the rabbit. "It sounded like a fox talking. I'm glad I didn't go away."

"So am I," said Grandfather Goosey, "for my daughter has gone on a visit, and I'm home all

alone, and I can't get myself anything to eat, and
I'm hungry—so hungry!"

"That's too bad!" cried Uncle Wiggily.
"But don't worry. I know the very thing for
you."

"What?" asked Grandfather Goosey.

"Pancakes—Buckwheat pancakes!" cried the
old gentleman rabbit. "Pancakes, with sausage
and maple syrup. Hot ones! I had some over
at the Wibblewobble house just now, and they're
fine!"

"But I can't go over to the duckhouse, sick
as I am," said Grandfather Goosey. "My cold
would be worse, and it's bad enough now, goodness knows," and he coughed and sneezed and
had a dreadful time for several minutes.

"But you don't need to go away," said Uncle
Wiggily. "I will make the cakes for you right
here."

"Can you make pancakes?" asked the duck
gentleman.

"Well, I have never tried it, but I watched
Mrs. Wibblewobble do it, and I'm sure I can,"
spoke Uncle Wiggily. "Now you just sit there
by the fire and I'll make the pancakes."

So he looked in the pantry, and he got some
buckwheat flour, and to make sure the cakes
would be nice he got another kind of flour, also,

and then he saw some grated cocoanut in a box
on the shelf, and he thought the cakes would be
better with some of that in.

So he put in some cocoanut, and then some
sugar and then some nutmeg and cinnamon, and
some butter and a little lard, and some Worces-
tershire sauce, and part of a can of tomatoes and
some condensed milk and a little honey, and then
he found a piece of cherry pie in his pocket, and
Uncle Wiggily put that in, too.

" There! " exclaimed the rabbit gentleman, as
he stirred all these things together in a pan, " I
guess these will be very good cakes."

" I should think they ought to," spoke Grandfather Goosey, with his feet still in hot water.
" You put enough stuff in them."

" Now, I'll bake them," said Uncle Wiggily,
so he put the griddle on the stove and greased it,
and when it was smoking hot he poured on some
of the pancake batter. Well, I just wish you
could have smelled the funny smell that happened
next. It was very queer, for Uncle Wiggily had
put a whole lot of wrong things in the pancakes,
you see and they burned.

" Hum! " said Grandfather Goosey. " That's
an odd smell."

" Yes, I guess something is wrong," said

Uncle Wiggily, puzzled-like. "Still they are griddle cakes and——"

And all of a sudden a big wolf jumped right in through the front door that Uncle Wiggily had left open.

"Griddle cakes or no griddle cakes!" cried the wolf, "I know what I am going to eat and it's going to be rabbit and duck!"

Then he made a spring for Uncle Wiggily.

"Oh, you are going to eat rabbit and duck are you?" cried Uncle Wiggily, and then as quickly as a flash of lightning he caught up the dish of pancake batter and he threw it all over that wolf. Into his eyes and nose and mouth it went, and it made him sneeze as if he had the whooping cough, and he ran out of Grandfather Goosey's house and wasn't seen afterward for a long time.

"Well, I got rid of him easily enough," said Uncle Wiggily proudly.

"Yes, but you have spoiled my pancakes," said the duck gentleman.

"Oh, I can easily make more pancakes," said the rabbit gentleman.

"Pancakes! You had better let me make them," said a voice and there stood Mrs. Wibble-wobble. She had come over to call on Grandfather Goosey, you see, not knowing Uncle Wiggily was there.

"Yes, I guess you had better make the cakes," spoke the rabbit. "Maybe I put in the wrong things," and he told Mrs. Wibblewobble what he had used.

"I should say it was wrong!" cried the duck lady with a laugh. "They would have been terrible funny pancakes." So she made some right ones for Grandfather Goosey, that were most delicious, and soon his cold was all better. Then Uncle Wiggily and Mrs. Wibblewobble went home in the auto.

And now if it doesn't rain snips and snails and puppy dogs' tails in the clothes basket, so the little mousie has no place to sleep, I'll tell you next about Uncle Wiggily in a snowstorm.

STORY XXIII

UNCLE WIGGILY IN A SNOWSTORM

" You don't mean to tell me that you are going out in your auto to-day, are you? " asked Mrs. Bow Wow one cold and stormy morning, when she saw Uncle Wiggily, the nice old gentleman rabbit, getting ready to go out to the barn where he kept his automobile. He had come to spend a little time with the Bow Wow dog family, you see.

" Oh, yes, I am going out for a little ride," said Uncle Wiggily, as he folded up his napkin, after having eaten about forty-'leven buckwheat cakes with sausage gravy and maple syrup. " I am going over to see Grandfather Goosey Gander."

" What! In all this storm? " asked Jackie Bow Wow, as he scratched his left ear with his left paw and looked to see if he had all his school books in his strap, for it was a Monday morning and almost school time.

" Oh, yes, this storm doesn't scare me," said
Uncle Wiggily, bravely. " I don't mind this a
bit. My automobile will just jump through between the snowflakes, and they won't hurt me at
all."

" No, I guess the snowflakes won't hurt you,"
spoke the little puppy dog, " but when they get
piled up into big banks and snowdrifts, can you
get through them? "

" I hope so," answered Uncle Wiggily.
" Anyhow, I am going away for a little while."

" But be sure and come back," begged Peetie
Bow Wow, the other puppy dog, " for Jackie
and I want to have some fun to-night after school,
and we want you to see it."

" Oh, I'll come back," said Uncle Wiggily.

Then Peetie and Jackie started off for school
with their books in straps over their shoulders.
And they had on their rubber boots and their big
overcoats, so they were very warm, though it was
a very cold day.

My! How the snow did come down, and the
wind blew the flakes every way, and up and down
and through the middle and into big piles and little piles. But Uncle Wiggily didn't mind this.
He waded out to the barn and then he looked at
his auto.

He found that the fizzilum-fazzilum was a little cold, so he lighted a match and warmed it, and then he put some gasoline in the tinkerum-tankerum, and he was ready to go off in the storm.

Well, he hadn't gone very far before he found that it was worse than he had thought it was. My! How the wind did blow! And how the snowflakes swirled about, beating into Uncle Wiggily's eyes and almost blinding him.

But he kept on, and the auto went choo-choo! as fast as anything, and soon the old gentleman rabbit was at the house where Grandfather Goosey Gander, the old gentleman duck, lived. Uncle Wiggily knocked on the door.

"Come on in!" cried Grandfather Goosey Gander. "I hope it is some friend of mine, so I can have some one to talk to."

"Yes, I'll talk to you and tell you all the news," said Uncle Wiggily. So he went in the duck gentleman's house and they sat by the fire and drank about forty-'leven cups of hot tea, and all the while the snowstorm was getting worse and worse, and the wind was blowing harder than ever.

"Well, I must start back," said Uncle Wiggily, after a little while. "I want to get home and see what fun Jackie and Peetie are going to have when they come from school."

So he said good-by to the old gentleman duck,
and gave him a piece of cherry pie, and then
Uncle Wiggily went out to his auto again, and
was soon on his way home.

But I just wish you could have seen that snowstorm. That is I do if you were warm and snug
in the house by the fire. Otherwise you would
have been very cold, and maybe you would have
turned into a snow man. Mind, I'm not saying
for sure, but maybe.

Uncle Wiggily was nearly turned into an
icicle, for the snow came down as he rode along
in his auto, and almost covered him up and made
him look like Santa Claus.

All the while his auto was moving along, but
it kept going slower and slower until finally it
ran into a big snowdrift and then, all of a sudden, it stopped altogether.

"Hum! That's funny!" cried Uncle Wiggily. "There must be something the matter with
the doodle-oodle-um." He tried to get out to
look at that part of the auto, but the snow was so
deep that when he stepped into it the old gentleman rabbit went in over his boot tops, right down
in a drift.

"I guess I'd better stay in the auto," he said,
as he got up on the seat again. "I'll see if I can't
make it go from here." So he turned and twisted

on the handles, and all at once the auto gave a
jump.

It jumped right ahead, and the wheels went
whizzing around and all at once the auto was
right in the middle of a big snowbank. There
poor Uncle Wiggily was, sitting in his auto, and
he was right inside of the snowdrift. There was
snow on top of him and snow under the wheels
of his auto, and on each side, just as if he were
in a snow house.

"Oh, my!" cried Uncle Wiggily. "This is
terrible. I wonder if I can get out of here?" So
he tried to make his auto go, but he couldn't because the snow was all up around the wheels.

"I'll have to stay here until warm weather
comes," thought the old gentleman rabbit, "and
by that time I'll freeze. Oh! I wish I had
stayed home, and not come out in the storm."

So he tried more and more to get out of the
snowbank, but he couldn't and finally he fell
asleep in his auto.

About this time Peetie and Jackie Bow Wow
came back from school. And when they heard
their mamma say that Uncle Wiggily wasn't
home yet they became frightened.

"Oh, maybe he's snowed in," said Jackie
sorrowfully.

"I believe he is," said Peetie. "We must dig him out."

So those two brave puppy dogs got their snow shovels and they went out in the storm, and pretty soon they came to the big snowbank under which was the old gentleman rabbit. Then they began to dig. And they dug and they dug, and the old fuzzy fox came along and tried to stop them, but they threw snow on him and he ran away. And then, after a while they dug down to where Uncle Wiggily was asleep in his auto, and Peetie's snow shovel tickled the old gentleman rabbit in the ribs and awakened him.

"Oh, how can I ever get home?" asked Uncle Wiggily, for he didn't know it was Peetie and Jackie.

"We have shoveled a path for you," said Jackie, and surely enough they had. Then the two doggie boys got in the auto and Uncle Wiggily started it off and he ran it along the snow path, until he was safely at the doggies' house and then it was supper time.

And after supper the puppy boys did tricks.

So that's how Uncle Wiggily was caught in a snowstorm and how Peetie and Jackie dug him out, and on the page after this, if the big cat in our back yard doesn't cry for a stick of lemon candy and wake the baby, I'll tell you about Uncle Wiggily and the snowball.

STORY XXIV

UNCLE WIGGILY AND THE SNOWBALL

ONE day there was another big snowstorm in the country where Uncle Wiggily, the nice old gentleman rabbit, was paying a visit to his two nephews, Peetie and Jackie Bow Wow, the puppy-dog boys. Oh, my! how the snow did come down, for it was almost Christmas time, you know, and it was real winter.

"Oh, we'll have a lot of fun!" cried Peetie to Jackie, as they got out of bed and looked from the window to see the big white flakes falling from the sky, just as if the old lady who lived in a shoe were sifting geese feathers out of a spring bed.

"Indeed we will have fun!" cried Jackie. "We'll build a snow fort, and have a snow battle, and we'll roll up a big snowball as big as our house!"

"Oh, but we have to go to school first," said Peetie, a little bit sadly. "Wouldn't it be nice if we could stay out all day?"

" It would," agreed the other little puppy dog boy, " but still maybe we can have some fun on our way to school, snowballing each other."

And, sure enough, they did have lots of fun. On their way to school they met Sammie Little-tail, the boy rabbit, and Jimmie Wibblewobble, the boy duck, and Johnnie and Billie Bushytail, the boy squirrels, and a lot of their other animal friends.

" Let's see who can throw the most snow-balls! " cried Peetie.

" I can," answered Johnnie Bushytail, and then, my goodness me and a basket of onions! Those boy animals had the best kind of fun! There were so many snowballs flying about through the air that it looked like two snow-storms made into one.

" Here come Lulu and Alice Wibblewobble! " cried Peetie Bow Wow, as he saw the duck girls on their way to school. " Let's wash their faces."

" But you mustn't do it very hard," objected Jimmie, their brother, for he was a very brave boy duck and loved his sisters.

" Oh, no, we wouldn't be impolite enough for that," spoke Peetie, and believe me they weren't a bit rough when they took pawsfull of snow and washed Lulu's and Alice's faces—but the duck girls screamed just the same, and the boys shouted and tumbled around in the snow, and they had lots of fun. And then the school bell rang and they had to go in to their lessons.

"Well, what shall we do; make a snow fort, or roll a big snowball?" asked Peetie when school was out.

"Make a snowball, take it to the tip-top of the hill, and let it roll down," suggested Jackie.

"All right!" cried all the others, so they started to do that.

The snow was just right for making big snow-balls, for it wasn't too hard nor too soft, and pretty soon Peetie and Jackie and Jimmie and Billie and Johnnie had rolled such a large snow-ball that I'm afraid to tell you just how immense it was for fear of scaring you. And they managed to get it right on top of a hill, and there they had to stop and rest, for they were quite tired.

"Now, what shall we do?" asked Jimmie, as he caught his breath, which nearly got away from him.

"Roll it down!" exclaimed Jackie. "If we all give it a push down it will go as fast as anything."

"Fine!" cried all the boy animals. So they pushed and pushed, and all of a sudden the snowball started rolling, and down the hill it rolled, almost as fast as a trolley car.

And then, all at once, Jackie cried out:

"Oh, my! Oh, dear! Oh, wow! Oh, hum, suz-dud!"

"Why, what is the matter?" asked his brother Peetie. "Don't you feel well? Have you a pain?"

"Oh, yes, I feel well enough," answered Jackie. "But look! That ball is rolling right down the hill and it's going to roll right up against the front stoop of Grandfather Goosey Gander's house, and maybe it will smash in the door. Oh, dear! Why did we do it? Why didn't we look before we rolled it? Why weren't we careful?"

And, as true as I'm telling you, that big snow-ball was rolling straight for Grandfather Goosey's house.

"Quick! Let's run after the snowball, and maybe we can stop it before it hits his door," suggested Jimmie. So they all ran after the rolling ball. But, bless your hearts! they could no more get it than you can catch a mosquito in summer, when he gets away from you.

And the next minute the snowball had hit Grandfather Goosey's front door with a " slam-bang!" and there it stayed, right on his front stoop. Why, the ball was so big that it hid the door from sight. Then all the boy animals who had rolled the ball down the hill came running up. Inside the house they could hear the old grandfather goose gentleman crying out:

"Oh, my! Oh, dear! What's that? Was it an earthquake that hit my house, or was it Uncle Wiggily in his auto? Oh, me; Oh, my!"

"It was our snowball," said Peetie sorrowfully.

Then Grandfather Goosey Gander looked from his window, and he saw the big snowball at his front door and he said:

"Oh, now I can't get out, and no one can come in, and I can't get anything to eat until that snowball melts, and I'll starve."

"Can't you come out the back door?" asked Jackie.

"There is no back door to my house," answered Grandfather Goosey. "It is nailed up for the winter. Oh, what shall I do? You boys will have to get that snowball away from my front door, somehow."

Well, those boys were frightened, and they tried their best to get the snowball away, but it was stuck fast and they couldn't move it. They didn't know what to do, and Grandfather Goosey was so excited in his house that he was jumping up and down on one leg, when, all of a sudden, along came Uncle Wiggily Longears in his auto. He saw what the trouble was right away, and got ready to help.

"Boys, get me the clothes line," he said. So Peetie and Jackie got it from Grandfather Goosey's back yard. Then Uncle Wiggily put the clothes line around the snowball, and then he tied one end of the line to his auto. Then he started off in the machine, "Ruff-puff!" and my goodness me sakes alive! That auto was so strong that it pulled the snowball off the front stoop as easily as a locomotive pulls a train of cars, and then Grandfather Goosey could come out and get something to eat.

"But don't roll any more big balls on my front steps, if you please, boys," he said, and they promised that they wouldn't.

Then they all went home from school, and so we'll rest a bit, if you please, but in case the girl hanging out the towels in the yard doesn't put a clothespin on her nose, to make herself look like an elephant, the next story will be about Uncle Wiggily and the picture book.

STORY XXV

UNCLE WIGGILY AND THE PICTURE BOOK

"WELL, where are you going to-day?" asked Mrs. Bow Wow, the puppy-dog lady, as she saw Uncle Wiggily, the nice old gentleman rabbit, giving his automobile a drink. You see the auto was thirsty after having pulled the big snowball off Grandfather Goosey's front stoop, as I told you in the story before this one. "Where are you going, Uncle Wiggily?" asked Mrs. Bow Wow again.

"Oh, I am just going to take a little ride through the woods, and call on Mrs. Bushytail, the squirrel lady," said Uncle Wiggily. "I want to see how her new baby is?"

What's that? Didn't I tell you before that Johnnie and Billie Bushytail had a little baby sister? Oh, yes they had. I believe, now that I think of it, that I did forget to mention it before. Yes, the little baby squirrel came around Hallowe'en time, and she was just as cute as she could be, and Uncle Wiggily just loved her, and so did every one else, of course.

"Well, if you go out riding you'll come back to Peetie and Jackie, won't you?" asked Mrs. Bow Wow. "They'll be so disappointed if you don't."

"Oh, yes, I'll come back," promised Uncle Wiggily. "I am just going to make a short visit, and I want to bring a little present to the new baby. I think I'll get her a picture book at the ten and five cent store."

"Oh, my!" exclaimed Mrs. Bow Wow. "Baby Friskie is too little to read books. Get Friskie a rattle box, Uncle Wiggily." You see the little squirrel's name was Friskie.

"No, I think I will get her a picture book," said the old gentleman rabbit. "Of course she can't read it now, but she can look at the pictures, and if I can find a book with real funny pictures in they will make her laugh instead of crying when she had a pain."

"Oh, you funny Uncle Wiggily!" exclaimed Mrs. Bow Wow, and she laughed, but still she knew the old gentleman rabbit was very kind-hearted.

So away Uncle Wiggily started for the ten and five cent store. It didn't take him very long to get there in his auto, and soon he had bought the picture book. Oh, it had such funny pictures in it! and they were colored very prettily.

They were so funny that Uncle Wiggily laughed as he looked at them, and then the girl behind the counter, she looked at them, and she laughed, too, and the girl next to her laughed and the boy who was wrapping up bundles laughed, and then Uncle Wiggily laughed so hard that he could hardly get his money out of his pocket, and soon the whole store full of people were laughing, and every one was happy.

Well, finally Uncle Wiggily managed to pay for the picture book, and he took it out to his auto with him, and once more he started off, this time for the squirrel house, where little baby Friskie lived. They called her that, you know, because she frisked about so lively. She was almost as lively as Jennie Chipmunk.

And now comes the sad part of the story, only it's not so very sad, and it doesn't last very long, and then it gets glad again. I just thought I'd tell you.

All at once, as Uncle Wiggily was going along through the woods in his auto, holding the picture book on his lap, and thinking how little Friskie would like it, all of a sudden, down out of the sky swooped a big fat blackbird. And with one grab of his bill he snatched that picture book off

Uncle Wiggily's lap and up into the air he flew with it.

"Oh, my! Come back with that, if you please!" cried the old gentleman rabbit. "That isn't good to eat, Mr. Blackbird."

"Well, when the blackbird found out that he had made a mistake, and that the book wasn't good to eat he felt so vexed (which means sort of angry, you know), he was so vexed that, what did he do but drop the pretty picture book down in a big hollow stump? It was a high stump, away over Uncle Wiggily's head, even when he stood up in the auto, and there the picture book was, where the rabbit gentleman couldn't get it. Then the blackbird flew away.

"Oh, my now! Isn't that a shame!" exclaimed Uncle Wiggily. "There's Friskie's book down in the hollow stump, and I haven't time to go back to the store for another. I don't see why that blackbird wanted to be so unpleasant. I wonder if I can get the book out?"

So he got down from his auto and tried to reach a stick down inside the stump, to fish up the book. But that wouldn't work.

"Perhaps I can run my auto against the stump hard enough to knock it down, and then I can get the book," said the rabbit gentleman, and as he tried that, making the auto go " ker-

bunk!" up against the hollow stump, but that
plan didn't work, for the stump was too strong.

Then Uncle Wiggily felt so badly about
Friskie's picture book that he didn't know what
to do, and he just sat there looking at the stump.
And then, all of a sudden, there was a rustling
in the bushes, and out came the skillery-scalery
alligator, with the double-jointed tail.

"Oh, dear!" cried Uncle Wiggily. "I'm
afraid I'm caught this time!" for you see he was
out of his auto, and the alligator was right close
to him, where he could grab Uncle Wiggily in a
minute. But what do you think happened?
Why, that alligator said, in the kindest voice in
the world:

"Don't be afraid, Uncle Wiggily. I'm not
bad any more. I wouldn't even hurt a baby
mosquito. I'm good now, so don't worry."

"Oh, I'm so glad!" cried the rabbit gentleman, as he made his ears go flip-flap.

"But why do you look so sad?" asked the
alligator. "You make me feel badly, too," and
the alligator cried some big tears that splashed
all over.

"I am sad because Friskie's picture book is
down inside that tall, hollow stump," said Uncle
Wiggily, sorrowful-like.

"Then don't be a bit sad any more," spoke the

alligator, "for with my rough, double-jointed tail, which is just like a saw, I will saw down that stump and you can get the book."

And would you ever believe it if I didn't tell you? But that skillery-scalery alligator did actually saw the tree stump down close to the ground with his double-jointed tail, and there, inside, was the picture book safe and sound, not hurt a bit, and Uncle Wiggily easily picked it up.

Then he thanked the good alligator very kindly, and took the book to Friskie, and oh! how pleased the baby squirrel was with it. And now I must stop for a while, but in case the baby doesn't cry any tears on my typewriter, and make it rusty and squeaky so that the sugar bowl bites a hole in the lemonade pitcher, I'll tell you next about Uncle Wiggily buying a new dress.

STORY XXVI

UNCLE WIGGILY BUYS A NEW DRESS

Now just wait a minute, if you please. If you have read the name of this story, as I suppose you have, or had some one read it for you, please don't jump up and say:

" Oh, there he goes again! Mixing things all up, as the stories do get lop-sided once in a while! " I'm sure I'm very sorry when anything goes wrong, but this time I am right. This story is to be about Uncle Wiggily buying a new dress. But listen! It was not for himself, for old gentlemen rabbits do not wear dresses, except in Greece, which is near Turkey. Uncle Wiggily bought that dress for—oh, well, I think I might as well start at the end and go right through to the beginning.

One morning Uncle Wiggily awakened in the nice hollow stump-house where he lived. He stretched his ears a bit, and then got up.

" Well," he exclaimed, making his red eyes twinkle like some pink lemonade at the circus, "well, I wonder what will happen to me to-day?"

For you see he was going to ride around in his auto so he would not get so fat, and nearly always something happened to him on these trips.

Well, this time he got up, looked out of the window, saw that it was going to be a fine day, and went down to his breakfast, which Nurse Jane Fuzzy-Wuzzy, the kind muskrat, had ready for him. I think it was candied apples, with oatmeal sauce on, this time. Uncle Wiggily ate as much as was good for him, and then he went out to feed his auto.

What's that? You didn't know autos ate anything? Why, of course they do. They have to have water to drink, and of course if an auto drinks it must eat. And once I saw a man pouring gasoline in his auto, and pretty soon that gasoline was all gone. And if the auto didn't eat it up I'd like to know what became of it, so I would.

Well, after Uncle Wiggily had fed and watered his auto, he went out for a ride. He had not gone very far before he passed the house where Mrs. Wibblewobble, the mother of Lulu, Alice and Jimmie, the duck children, lived.

Mrs. Wibblewobble was waving her left wing
as fast as she could.

" Oh dear! " she cried.

" What is the matter? " asked Uncle Wiggily. " Is the house on fire? "

" No," answered the duck lady, " but I want
to go to a party that Aunt Jerushia Ann, the
dear, little, nervous old lady woodchuck is going
to give, and I haven't a new dress to wear to it."

" Why, go buy one! " exclaimed Uncle Wiggily. " I am rich, here is the money," and he put
his paw in his pocket.

" Oh, no, no! " cried Mrs. Wibblewobble
quickly. " I have the money right here," and she
showed where she kept it under her right wing.
" But the trouble is that I have no time to go
shopping. I have to bake a pie and a cake and
a pudding, and wash and scrub the dishes, so I
have no time to go to the five and ten cent store
and buy my dress. And I do so want to look
nice at the party! "

" Ha! Hum! " exclaimed Uncle Wiggily.
" I do not blame you. Look here! Do you
think I could buy that dress for you? "

" Of course you could, if you will be so kind,"
replied Mrs. Wibblewobble, making her yellow
bill open in a smile. " I want a lilac shaded
charmeuse, with polnaise trimming down the

side, with fur around the upper edges and some
dingle-dangles on the corners. Then there must
be some faloodles on the sleeves, and——"

"Stop, stop, please!" begged Uncle Wiggily.
"I can't remember all that. I'll write it down."

So he did on a piece of white birch bark, and
then off he went in his auto to the five and ten
cent store to buy the new dress. When he got
in the store a nice little mousie clerk, who had
soap and perfumery and combs and brushes and
all things like that to sell, asked of the rabbit
gentleman:

"What do you wish to buy?"
"A new dress," he replied.
She looked at him funny-like.
"Oh, I don't want it for myself!" exclaimed
Uncle Wiggily quickly. "It's for Mrs. Wibble-
wobble, the duck lady."

"Well," said the nice little mousie clerk, "you
go over that way two aisles, and then down three
aisles, over two more aisles, turn to your right,
go up one pair of stairs, and down two pair of
stairs; jump over the door sill and there are the
dresses. Then you——"

"Wait—wait!" begged Uncle Wiggily. "I
never can remember all that. I must write it
down."

So he did on the same piece of birch bark that he had used to write down what Mrs. Wibblewobble told him about the dress.

Well, after getting lost two or three times, and wandering about the piano department and the grocery division, Uncle Wiggily got to where the dresses were sold.

A nice little froggie girl clerk waited on him.

"I want," said Uncle Wiggily, "a new dress, with soap trimmings on the charmeuse front, with gores on the faloodles, and slashed up and down the middle aisle, then it must have satin in the piano department, and phonographs on the train. Back of the dingle-dangles there is to be a polonaise and hobble skirt."

"That is a funny dress," said the froggie girl. "Is it for yourself?"

"For Mrs. Wibblewobble," answered Uncle Wiggily.

"Very well, I think I have just what you want," said the five and ten cent store clerk, and she was so kind that she never told Uncle Wiggily he had everything all mixed up. But that clerk knew he had, all the same. There was never a dress like that.

So finally the dress was wrapped up, and Uncle Wiggily took it in his auto with him to go to Mrs. Wibblewobble so she could wear it to the party. And on the way the rabbit gentleman opened the package to look at the dress.

"Oh, what a beauty!" he cried, as he saw the Ethel Rose colored ribbons on the seams.

Then, all of a sudden out from the bushes, jumped an elephant, with a long trunk and flapping ears. And he was a very mad elephant because no one had given him peanuts that day.

"Oh, bur-r-r-r! Wow!" the elephant cried. "I am going to break your auto all to pieces!" and he stood right in front of it so Uncle Wiggily could go no farther.

"Why, pray, will you do that?" asked the rabbit gentleman gently.

"Because I am bad, I suppose," answered the elephant cross-like.

Well, he was just going to smash that auto with his trunk, and for no good reason at all, when, all at once there came a gust of wind, and it blew Mrs. Wibblewobble's new dress out of the paper right over Uncle Wiggily's head, so that it looked exactly as if he were wearing it.

The elephant looked on in surprise.

"Oh, I beg your pardon!" he exclaimed. "I did not see at first that you were a lady. I never bother the ladies, nor break their autos. I will do you no harm. Good day. I will go off and break a stone."

And off he went and Uncle Wiggily was saved, because the elephant thought he was a lady, all on account of the new dress the rabbit gentleman had bought. So it is a good thing Uncle Wiggily went shopping for the duck lady; isn't it?

So we have come to the end of this book, for, you can see for yourself there isn't room for another story in it. And if I write any more about the rabbit gentleman I shall have to put the stories in another book. So I'll say good-bye until that book comes out.

THE END.